ZOMBIE KILLER HANDBOOK

2nd Illustrated Edition

by

Frank Jardim

Preface

If you are reading this little book, it's likely you have a fascination with post apocalyptic fiction. I do too. It started with films like Panic in the Year Zero and Day of the Triffids, and later George Romero's The Crazies and Night of the Living Dead. By the time Romero's excellent sequels to the 1968 original came out, I was hooked for life. Unfortunately, most other zombie apocalypse fiction that I've watched and read has left me wishing I hadn't. They often start out with a good idea and then flop in the execution. The worst offense is a failure to believably ground the story in the real world, governed as it is by laws of nature and human behavior. As I wrote these fictional essays, I tried to have reality always on my mind. However, I did not write this book to be a crusader for plausible zombie apocalypse fiction. The truth is I wrote this book by accident.

The real motivation behind these essays was to set the stage in the muddy waters of the zombie apocalypse genre for a shooting sports venture I began in the winter of 2011. I've been a recreational shooter since I was ten years old and around 2008 I became aware of zombie apocalypse themed shooting matches around the country. This looked really fun on the surface in light of my interests but turned out to be a big disappointment when I realized all the competitors shot at was paper and steel targets that didn't even look like zombies in most cases. I decided that I would make a zombie shooting match worthy of the name and created Zombie Shooters United LLC, or ZSU for short. I designed and built my own realistic, life-size, reactive zombie targets that would only fall with a shot to the brain. These targets, along with story driven competition stages in real world settings make for the most unique and exciting tactical shooting experience a zombie apocalypse genre fan can have. Finally, you too can fight your way through a George Romero zombie movie.

These essays were designed to help our shooters prepare for and successfully compete in the matches. I was originally going to publish them on our website for free but my wife said, "No way! You spent two months writing that. You aren't going to give it away." So, this book was really her doing.

What you see before you now, is a new illustrated edition of Zombie Killer Handbook, published after a full year of our ZSU zombie shooting matches. The photographs you see are my actual targets and my competitors. If this sort of thing appeals to your inner zombie killer, I hope you'll visit www.ZombieShootersUnited.com and join us on Facebook at Zombie Shoot and YouTube at ZombieKillerSooZ. You can even join ZSU, and if you like, start an affiliated club in your town. In any case, I hope you enjoy the book.

Introduction to Zombie Killer Handbook

After a viral zombie apocalypse decimates the world population in 2012, a rural Kentucky city (Elizabethtown) is transformed into a fortress for humanity thanks to the combined efforts of survivors from the region. Taking the name Live-E-town, this survivor enclave stands up a force of contracted Zombie Killers to protect itself. Known as ZKs, these resourceful mercenaries defend Live E-town's borders and make war on the undead and human raider bands that inhabit the dangerous Dead Zones. By 2014, Live E-town's ZKs are the dominant living force in the Dead Zones in a hundred mile range. Their offensive operations have pushed a perimeter out five miles into the farmland surrounding the town, diverted and exterminated scores of undead herds, suppressed most of the raider groups, rescued thousands of survivors, and recovered hundreds of tons of survival critical resources. Live E-town is a beacon of hope for mankind's continued existence but survival remains a daily battle, the outcome of which has yet to be determined. The war to take the world back from the undead is only in its initial engagements.

The Zombie Killer Handbook is a guide for offensive operations against the undead written by a pragmatic, knowledgeable combatant. It was published in Live E-town in late 2014 as a training manual for new recruits to the contract ZK force. It is a collection of essays written by a well known and highly regarded ZK on the equipment, weapons, tactics, missions and threats in the Dead Zones.

The essays are all reluctantly authored by a famed, and perhaps infamous, ZK Captain called Soo-Z. Little of this unlikely pony-tailed heroine's life before the apocalypse is revealed but it becomes apparent that she is Asian born, of slight stature, not out of her 20s, solitary and guarded in personality, deeply religious and violent in temperament and action to the extent that would be alarming anytime other than a zombie apocalypse. Nobody knows why she was in Kentucky when the apocalypse took place but she distinguished herself in the pivotal battles that saved Elizabethtown and afterward carried the fight to its undead (and living) enemies with messianic zeal. She is in charge of the ZKs stationed at Outpost #7 on the eastern perimeter and is as much feared as respected. Soo-Z's essays get to the crux of matters quickly with experience based knowledge and authority and surprising humor. Beyond the fascinatingly detailed accounts of the ZKs harrowing work in the Dead Zones, they give the reader a glimpse of the sensibilities and values of a post-apocalyptic survivor turned warrior.

ZOMBIE KILLER HANDBOOK

Confidential

(This handbook was compiled from a series of essays prepared by the respected ZK Captain Soo-Z specifically to provide valuable guidance to new contract zombie killers.   The contents of this handbook are not for general distribution to the survivor population. All copies are numbered for tracking purposes.   Should your copy be discovered out of your possession, you may be subject to disciplinary action. In order to expedite publication, no effort was made to censor or edit the essays which were originally written on a weekly basis and distributed to ZKs on outpost duty with their Dead Zone intelligence reports.   The essays were re-organized to group related subjects and hopefully add clarity.)

Issued to:____   Copy #_________

Table of Contents

Introduction from Capt. Soo-Z

Greeting New ZKs,

Those of you that know me at all know that I am not much for conversation. Don't take this the wrong way. Outside of our professional relationship as contract zombie killers, I have no interest whatsoever in any of you, on any level. If you are getting married, it's your birthday, you don't like rice, your girlfriend is cheating on you, you hate cats…I don't care. Don't tell me about this stuff because it will only make me angry. If you think I'm not nice *(and I don't care if you do)* you should see me when I'm angry. At Outpost #7 we eat a lot of rice. I like rice. Most Asians do. If you don't like rice… tough crap. Go in the forest and forage for truffles or start a potato patch. At Outpost #7 we have a cat. I don't care if you don't like cats. I don't like this cat either. He or she is here to keep Outpost #7 mouse-free. I hate mice almost as much as I hate zombies. You will treat the cat in the manner cats like to be treated so it doesn't run away and you will clean the beast's litter box. So much for our formal introduction. Maybe you are hoping you don't get assigned to Outpost #7. Naturally, I don't care.

The reason I am writing this is the Mayor of Live E-town asked me to prepare a series of essays on subjects related to the ZK profession that may be helpful in your survival and subsequent professional development. I've been doing this longer than anyone I know (that is still alive anyway) and he thinks I have something of value to convey to you. After I declined, he offered me considerable financial remuneration for my effort. Since a girl has to look out for herself, I agreed. I'll write on one or two subjects each week until I feel I can get out of writing any more. I suppose you can ask questions but I will not answer them if they are stupid. The first lecture will be on Choosing Primary Weapons.

Confusion to the enemy!

Capt. Soo-Z

P.S. I've noticed people spelling my name in a lot of startling ways. However you semi- literates spell it, know that it is pronounced "sue-see." Yes, that's short for Susan, which is my Christian name. Unless you are Jesus, you call me Captain Soo-Z.

My old shingle, before I went contract for Live E-town.

Am I cut out to be Zombie Killer? Soo-Z helps you rate your relative Bad-Assness.

There's bad-ass and there's really bad-ass, and I've seen it all. To be a good ZK It takes a certain… je ne sais pas? Oh yeah… bad-ass. Those without it need not apply. You're embarrassing yourself and it actually hurts the rest of us to watch it. You could also get one of us killed. That is unacceptable. If a ZK gets to meet his maker, it's supposed to be in a knife fight over a rigged zombie exhibition fighting match, a moonshine still explosion or falling off the roof while trying to rescue Blackie or whatever the Outpost #7 cat is named. ZK's don't get their comrades killed for lack of bad-ass. So here's a simple test for you to rate yourself and save everybody a lot of trouble.

1. Three zombies come crashing into your front yard while you are eating your evening meal with your woman (or man) and minor children *(of your own loins or another's it matters not.)* You do which of the following?

> a. Rush everyone to safety in the cellar and lock yourselves in. *(Prudent, but not even a little bad-ass.)*
> b. Excuse yourself from the table and head for the door to greet them picking up a shotgun on the way. *(More genteel than bad-ass. Shows good upbringing.)*
> c. Excuse yourself from the table and head for the door to greet them with only your chopsticks. *(Now we're talking bad-ass.)*
> d. Excuse yourself from the table saying "Baby, I'm taking this to go." and head for the door with your chop sticks and rice bowl. *(Off-the-chart bad-ass!)*

2. Your five man ZK patrol is taking small arms fire from all sides from the upper stories of ruined buildings in Dead Louisville. Your captain yells to you, "We're surrounded by raiders!" You immediately think to yourself which of the following?

> a. Maybe I should try to surrender? *(Yikes! Hope you like getting raped in every hole before you die.   That cat at the outpost, Blackie or whatever, is less of a pussy than you.)*
> b. I'm going to get as many of these fuckwads as I can before

they kill me. *(Unless you're picking up and throwing their own grenades right back at them, this is not particularly bad-ass. Even a bunny will fight when cornered.)*
c. They've got us surrounded…the poor bastards. *(That's pretty damn bad-ass any day of the week.)*
d. After I feed these shitheads their own dicks, I got to scrounge around here for a new DVD player so the kids at the Heartland Montessori School can watch those Animal Planet DVDs. *(Too bad-ass to measure with any known metrics.)*

3. It is a clear, dry morning and you are driving an F-150 pick-up truck equipped with a snowplow at 45mph down a partially cleared section of Route 62 outside the perimeter on a run to resupply some of your team's safe houses. About a mile ahead you see two zombies walking on opposite sides of the road. What do you do?

a. Pass them by rather than risk damaging the truck and getting stuck in the Dead Zone.
(I guess you thought the "Z" and "K" on the patch we wear stood for "zesty kumquat".)
b. Hit the one on the right since he's on the way. *(You call that bad-ass? I call it just plain lazy. You appear to be an underachiever.)*
c. Plow the one on the right. Hit the brakes. Throw it in reverse, and let the one in you left side mirror eat some tailgate at 25mph. *(I am willing to acknowledge you as a peer.)*
d. Slow down a little, engage the PTO and adjust the plow angle, disengage the PTO and speed up to 55mph to hit the zombie on the right and launch him across the road with enough velocity to re-kill the zombie on the left side too. *(Holy shit! Pulling off a classic   7-10 split on the highway demonstrates nearly God-like bad-assness. Also, I want you on the Outpost #7 Bowling Team.)*

4. You are on your own searching for survivors in a once quite exclusive private golf course. While sweeping the second story bar of the posh club you look out the window to see at least a hundred undead gathering outside, ostensibly for their 10am tee-off time. They see you and decide on brunch instead. What do you do?

a. Secure the stairway doors to your floor, lay low and try to wait them out. *(Sure hope some sharp eyed ZK realizes you are in there when they sweep back through this area. The zombies certainly won't forget you.)*

b. Secure the stairway doors to your floor. Make a lot of noise to try to draw as many as possible inside the club. Open a window, lower yourself down with a table cloth rope and try to make a run for it. *(A solid plan but a hundred zombies hanging around makes an otherwise classy place look kind of lowbrow. You disappoint me.)*

c. Secure the stairway doors to your floor. Make a lot of noise to try to draw as many undead as possible inside the club. Set the joint on fire with some Bacardi 151 rum Molotov cocktails from the bar. Open a window, lower yourself down with a table cloth rope and beat feet out of there while the burning undead golfers and their clubhouse provide a smoke screen to conceal your egress. *(Finally some much needed bad-ass. You wouldn't want to be in any club that would have you as a member anyway.)*

d. Secure the stairway doors. Chop a head size hole in the bottom of the door with your hand axe. Refine your golf swing as you drive about a hundred zombie brains across the bar with woods, irons, wedges, etc., while humming the Kenny Loggins song "I'm Alright." Leave one zombie alive to caddy for you. Take a set of clubs. Play 9 holes. Finish 3 under par. *(You have literally jackknifed a tractor trailer load of bad-ass here…and shot a great game of golf.)*

Scoring:

Give yourself 1 point for every letter "a" answer you chose.
Give yourself 2 points for every letter "b" answer you chose.
Give yourself 3 points for every letter "c" answer you chose.
Give yourself 4 points for every letter "d" answer you chose.

What it all boils down to:

4-7 pts. You're just a regular person, with normal fears and worries and doubts. You are capable of both bravery and cowardice depending on the circumstances. Bad-ass is not the word I'd use to describe you but I bet you've had your moments. *(Better stick to farming.)*

8-11 pts. You're a game scrapper. You are probably blessed with more luck than sense or talent. You might actually think you are bad-ass but you're really just jumping to reach bad-ass's lowest hanging fruit. If you live long enough, you might learn enough to become bad-ass naturally like coal turns to diamonds. *(We'll consider you for a ZK in the absence of better candidates and in times of pressing need.)*

12-15 pts. You are definitely bad-ass. You are the epitome of coolness under fire. You are so experienced that fear for you is just a little tingle that warns you when some shit is about to go down. You are a natural leader who does what needs to be done with efficiency and without reservation. Your unshakeable confidence scares the shit out of your enemies and inspires your comrades. *(You're hired!)*

16 pts. I've heard it said that it's a fine line between genius and madness. Buddy, if you are this bad-ass you could be insane. *(You might have a deity complex or something.)* People are initially drawn to you because of your God-like invulnerability and fearlessness but soon distance themselves. It doesn't matter to you one way or the other because you are probably a loner anyway. When you decide to take on an army of the undead with your bare hands because they are blocking the most direct path to the Blockbuster Video store, you can't figure on a lot of people sticking by your side. *(You may be officer material. Apply for a commission at the mayor's office.)*

ZK Speks before he went contract. The Elvis glasses alone would qualify as bad-ass but add extra bad-ass for having the kid watch his back and carry his smokes.

Running into 17 to 1 odds? That's what bad-ass looks like.

ZK Bloodi Mari setting up a hat-trick. Why? Because she's bad-ass.

Primary Weapons of the ZK: Longarms

Many of you have asked what type of clothing, weapons and equipment I use. Off duty it consists of a simple cheongsam and a Smith & Wesson 649 snubnose revolver. On duty, I dress for the weather and pack for the mission. There's a lot to this subject so I'll break it down. When it comes to a primary weapon, it's always going to be a longarm and preferably an autoloader. I'm small so I prefer lighter, graceful weapons. My favorite of late is the M2 carbine. The 110 gr. bullets have plenty of power out to 100 yards and take up no more space than 5.56mm NATO. I've got plenty of 15 and 30 round magazines for it. I've passed up a dozen ARs in various configurations because I just don't see the need for the bulk. They are fine weapons, but they are twice as big as they need to be and I look ridiculous carrying one. I can also shoot the M2 carbine with one hand. That's more important than you would expect. The full auto capability of the M2 is something I've used only once, and that was at 10 yards against living raiders. Against zombies it would be a total waste of precious .30 carbine ammo which isn't too common. I recover my spent cases when I can to reload them.

When it comes to ammo, pick soft-point hunting ammo over military full-metal-jacket every time you are lucky enough to have a choice. The expansion *(mushrooming)* that soft-point and hollow-point bullets offer in the best of circumstances works to your advantage. The more brain matter your bullet disrupts, the better the chances of killing the zombie. They work pretty well on live raiders too. From what I understand, the armies of the old world agreed to ban the more destructive soft-point hunting ammo from the battlefield in favor of full-metal-jacket (FMJ) for humanitarian reasons. With humanity's days looking like they may be numbered, I have no use for the quaint rationale of long dead generals. Neither should you. Use the bullet that expands the most and does the most tissue damage. The only caveat to that is the ammo must feed reliably in your rifle. Bolt action rifles happily chamber anything but the autoloaders can be finicky. Make sure you can clear a jammed cartridge quickly and efficiently because your life may depend on it.

One last thought on ammo. Don't waste your time carrying any military surplus armor piecing (AP) ammo. Theoretically this might come in handy if we are ever attacked by raiders driving cars, but

that hasn't happened yet. I bet it won't for the foreseeable future.
The AP ammo *(M855 is the commonly encountered U.S. Army
5.56mm AP cartridge and SS109 is the NATO equivalent)* is no
better than FMJ on human tissue. In my opinion it has the distinct
downside of causing collateral damage by continuing to make holes
in the things behind the zombies and raiders you want to make holes
in. The hardened penetrators inside AP ammo seem to be drawn by
some strange magnetism to hit and ruin the very supplies and
equipment we want to salvage in the Dead Zone. *(ex. radios,
propane tanks, tires, etc.)* I am convinced AP ammo is jinxed.

I carry all my extra ammo in a shoulder bag loaded in magazines
ready to use. If you have to change mags, the situation is usually
serious and zombies don't wait politely for you to refill them. I keep
45 to 60 rounds on me all the time *(a pair of 15 round mags in the
pouch on my belt and a 15 or 30 round mag in the gun)*. That way I
can drop the extra ammo load if I need to travel light and still be
ready for all but a siege. Of course, I rarely miss... except at night.

To make the carbine better at night, I taped a small LED
flashlight to the foregrip to light up my front sight. I got a good
sight picture through the rear aperture and illuminated close targets
at the same time. It was low tech but it worked at close range. The
big problem was the cheap light was too fragile and I noticed that it
wouldn't stay on reliably. It was an expedient until I found a
beautifully rugged Brownells BVL280 tactical flashlight. It's solid
enough to penetrate a skull if used as a hand weapon and the light is
intense and long range. I'm having it mounted on my carbine.
Scoop up whatever Brownells stuff you find in the Dead Zone. I've
found it uniformly excellent.

Realistically, most of your shots are going to be less than 50
yards. If you are more than 50 yards away from a zombie, chances
are you can remain unseen and not have to engage. The brain is a
pretty small target at 50 yards, some smaller than others, and there is
a lot to be said for telescopic sights. I'll admit; I like scopes. Both
the conventional optical glass type and the more resent battery
powered red dot type are great for longer shots, novice shooters and
people with poor eyesight.

The common glass optical hunting rifle scope usually has great
magnification *(up to 22X)*. Most seem to be between 6X and 9X
and often have variable magnifications. It can be tricky finding
your target at high magnification because your field of view through

the lens of the scope is pretty limited. It comes to you with practice.
An accurate rifle with a scope is a great tool to thin a herd of the
undead from a safe distance. Brain shots at 150 yards are no
problem for decent marksman. I'll generally keep my best rifle
shooter watching over us from a protected position with a 3X-9X
power scoped rifle, less for zombies than for raiders. The downside
of traditional telescopic sights is you have to be careful not to break
them, knock them out of alignment, or soak them in the rain and fog
them up.

The battery powered "red dot" scopes or "heads-up sights" are
much better for targets closer in. They usually don't have much
magnification and some don't have any. They are better in low light
encounters than the optical glass scopes and considerably more
durable. These scopes were favored by the military and some
represented pretty cutting edge technology just before the
apocalypse. I think they are terrific. They let a naturally clumsy
rifle like the M16 get on target very quickly. It will be a mournful
day indeed when the batteries finally run out. Make sure your iron
sights are zeroed.

Regardless of what type of longarm a ZK carries, you need to
have a sling to carry it on the march. I used different styles and
prefer a simple shoulder sling to a single point sling. The traditional
shoulder sling keeps the weapon secure against my body when I
walk, climb or run. I hate single point slings. When you have to
beat feet out of a deteriorating situation, the last thing any ZK needs
is their unfettered rifle flying around and getting tangled in their
legs, or worse, knocking them cold. I've seen this happen. A
traditional sling aids in accurate shooting too.

This carbine of mine has a bayonet lug but I don't have the
bayonet. Sometimes I dream I find the bayonet. These are happy
dreams. The bayonets, like the gun itself, were antiques before the
apocalypse. I have come to grips with the grim reality that I will
probably never find one. I now fill this emptiness in my soul with
lychee fruit on those occasions I come across an Asian food store.
Lychee fruit is good but a bayonet would still be a handy item in a
pinch. I wouldn't want to overuse it and bend the carbine's slim
barrel. Most military rifles have the capacity for a bayonet. Be on
the lookout for the bayonets.

The carbine also has a steel buttplate. I busted open more than a
few skulls with it. This is often quite messy but strangely

gratifying. It saves ammo when you must deliver the coup de grace to a crippled zombie or raider. One piece of advice when using your longarm's buttstock in this manner...keep your mouth closed.

Next time we talk handguns...selection criteria, marksmanship and the stupid things people think they can do with them even though there hasn't been any TV or movies to remind them for the last two years.

ZK McConn dropping zombies at 75 yards with an AK-47. The rifle shoots well enough for head shots at that range. Poor military ammo and a creepy trigger holds the AK-47 back from its potential. Many will shoot a lot better with good ammo.

Bullpup rifles are fast handling and very compact but almost need optics to overcome their short sight radius.

Pistol caliber carbines do good work in the Dead Zone. This fast shooting .44 magnum lever action is devastating on zombies and recoil is not bad.

The vintage M1 carbine is almost tailor made for zombie killing.

AR-15 platforms of are very popular among ZKs because of their light weight, high magazine capacity and tactical versatility, but you must keep them clean! The 5.56mm round is great for zombie killing too.

Sidearms: Secondary Weapons, But Not By Much

At close range, especially indoors, a ZK needs a handgun. In the field you need one hand free while you are searching, climbing or moving through debris. A medium caliber handgun is your best choice for protection in that scenario. Most ZK will carry handguns in the range of .38 to .45 caliber with 9mm being the most popular because the ammo is so common. They all do a good job. 9mm autoloaders often have a large capacity magazine and having 13 to 17 rounds on your hip is more comforting than the six rounds you find in the average revolver. If the zombies are close enough for you to use your pistol on, they are too damn close! Most of us have had the experience of opening a door and releasing a swarm of undead. That situation calls for quick recovery of your sight picture and target between shots and lightening fast reloads when you are out.

A 9mm or .40 cal. autoloader offers quick shooting and plenty of power to disrupt the zombies' grey matter. The .357 and .44 magnums are overkill. Their recoil, report and muzzle blast are pretty severe and can be tough to handle one handed. I haven't seen anyone that can shoot these cannons as fast and accurately as a medium caliber. I've found putting a 9mm or .38 Special into the part of the skull that encloses the brain generally blows a good chunk out the exit hole and the energy transfer stirs up the remaining brain tissue and shuts it down for good.

When possible, use plain, unjacketed, soft lead bullets. This is what the Ammunition Reloading Station back at Live E-town issues to ZKs. These soft bullets mushroom nicely and make a bigger hole inside than outside. Some guys make what they call a "dum-dum bullet" by cutting a fairly deep "X" in the tip of the bullet so it will fragment inside the brain. I haven't tested this but they appear to work as well as standard ammo. Also consider jacketed soft point ammo and hollow point bullets if they will feed reliably from your autoloading pistol's magazine. Your last choice should be full-metal-jacket (also called ball) ammo. The full-metal-jacketed bullets don't give you any added killing power since they don't expand like the others sometimes do.

The .22 long rifle cartridge is great for practice and training but I've observed that it often won't drop a zombie without perfect shot placement or multiple hits. About half the time it penetrates both sides of the skull but I've never seen it blow anything out the exit wound. I suspect that it isn't transferring enough energy to short circuit what's left of the zombie's brain function. The shots that seem to drop them are the ones that are either at or just above the eyes, passing through the brain stem. Additionally, you won't always be shooting zombies. The living are far more dangerous and hard to kill. Nobody hunts a man with a squirrel gun unless he is desperate or a fool. If you are stuck with a .22 long rifle pistol, try to have a lot of ammo.

You might wonder why I carry a revolver if fast reloading is so important. I keep my extra ammo in speed loaders in a pouch on the front of my belt. If I didn't have those speed loaders I wouldn't carry a revolver. That being said, here are two more reasons I choose this revolver. The first and most important is my 6" barrel S&W Model 10 is extremely accurate. *(The fixed sights can't get bumped out of alignment or broken off either.)* Some guns just shoot straighter than others. Find the most accurate one you can get that is still reliable. This brings me to the second reason. My revolver, like most, is 100% reliable. If it doesn't go bang, I just pull the trigger again. I've seen guys get bit because their auto-loading pistol jammed.

Live E-town's arsenals are trying to build up a stock of silenced handguns for issue to ZKs, at least on a limited basis, because of the advantage suppressed weapons offer. The undead can hear, see and smell us, in that order of sensitivity. A silenced shot is not likely to attract a swarm of undead to the search area which makes my job a lot easier. I've personally cleared an entire strip mall solo using a pair of silenced .45 ACP Colt Commanders. I still grieve the loss of these two pistols in a fire last July. A silenced handgun in any caliber is a really nice thing to have. I'm convinced they save lives.

The last thing I want to say on this subject concerns how you carry your handgun. Most of the accidental shootings I've seen involved handguns. Two ZK in the past two years accidentally and fatally shot themselves in the chest while re-holstering auto-loading pistols in a shoulder holster. That's just a stupid way to go. I use a hip holster, and a flapped one at that. Quick draw was never once a factor in the 250+ engagements I've fought in. It makes more sense to keep your handgun protected from loss and the weather. These days, if I meet someone with a concealed weapon, it indicates to me that they are up to no good. Honest people have no reason to hide their weapons. At least not their main weapons.

Here's my handgun rules in bullet form:
- You must have a handgun! Use whatever you got until something better comes along.
- Seek accuracy and reliability.
- Favor medium calibers that you can find! .38 Super and .45 Colt are great rounds but odds are you are not going to scrounge much ammo for them in the Dead Zones.
- Have a speedy means of reloading *(extra magazines or revolver speed loaders).*
- Carry your handgun in a covered hip holster to protect it and you.
- Get a silencer for your autoloader if you can.

Next Subject: Bludgeons & Blades: Weapons for close combat with the undead.

Revolvers can't be beat for reliability but you can get killed in the time it takes to reload them. A New York reload might be your best strategy if you lack speed-loaders.

An autoloader from 9mm to .45 ACP will help rack up the kills for you.

Keep your cool and let them come to you if the tactical situation permits. You are safer if you fight them in the open where you have room to maneuver.

Know your pistol intimately. Reloading needs to be smooth and fast. Imagine what could have happened here if you dropped your fresh magazine in the brush.

I've seen ZK Doc Boyd use a .22 LR pistol successfully on many occasions. It requires precise shot placement!

17% of Live E-town Zombie Killers are female. About 75% of them are as good or better than their male counterparts. The other 25% are so good you'd think they were perfect instruments of God's will.

Pistols are very useful in close quarters like indoors or in heavy forest or brush as is the case for ZK Kiwacka above. The most competent ZKs will make 25 yard headshots with their sidearms. That means they can drop the zombie in the yellow shirt on the far right in less time than it takes to tell it.

Shotguns: Specialty Weapon for ZKs & Arm of Choice for the Untrained Masses

I have a love-hate relationship with shotguns. In certain situations, they are exactly the weapon to have. Every other time they put you at a disadvantage.

In general, the positive aspects of shotguns include:
- Great stopping power.
- Require less precise aim than a rifle or handgun.

The negative aspects generally include:
- Short range
- Small ammunition capacity requires frequent reloading.
- Heavy recoil in larger gauges.
- Physical size and weight of shotgun ammo limits the amount you can carry.

Shotguns have accounted for a lot of undead. That's mostly because they were in a majority of homes and available for use when all hell broke loose. The close range encounters you have inside a building are one of the situations where a shotgun is terrific. Use them if the undead have gotten into your building or you have to enter a building to clear them out. The spread of the pellets increases your chances of destroying the brain. This is a real advantage when you have to fight in low light or poor visibility. *(ex. smoke, fog, high grass, dense forest or underbrush, etc.)* The shooter's aim doesn't have to be as precise so shotguns are great for the untrained, uncoordinated or vision impaired. They have great stopping power and even non-lethal hits to the body can knock the undead off their feet and buy the shooter time. You need time on your side with a shotgun. You need all the time you can get to reload it. Ammunition capacity varies with model from 1 to 6 rounds with most sporting models having a 3 round capacity.

Shotgun performance depends on ammunition selection too. Whenever possible, keep it loaded with 00 buckshot. There aren't as many pellets, but each one is like a .32 caliber bullet and these rounds are pretty hotly loaded. A couple of those bigger pellets hitting the brain simultaneously scrambles it nicely, usually blowing chunks of it out of the skull. I've blown off door locks with 00 buckshot. *(At point blank range all ammunition acts the same because the pellets have no chance to spread out into their pattern. They hit the target in a near solid blob of lead.)*

If you are farther away and you have a short barreled shotgun, or something less than a full choke on your long barrel shotgun, you will find that the tiny birdshot pellets spread out so much you can't reliably get enough of them in the brain to destroy it. Most of the zombie brain is dead already. To stop it you need to destroy the little bit that still works. Destroying the part that's already dead doesn't help much. Save your birdshot rounds for hunting for food. Kill zombies with 00 buckshot.

Without knowing the variables of barrel length, choke and ammunition type, it's hard to be specific about shotgun performance. Here's a baseline observation to work from. A shotgun with a 28" barrel with full choke shooting 00 buckshot will consistently kill zombies at 65' range if your aim is good. Birdshot at that range is ineffective. If you are stuck with a short tactical shotgun *(18-20" improved cylinder bore barrel)* you are going to need to get a lot closer.

In a building, that short barrel is an advantage because it's handier than a long barreled turkey gun and most of your shots are less than 30'. In the high grass or woods you might be better off with a longer barrel gun. That long barrel is useful as a prod to hold the undead off of you while you reload… as long as there aren't too many.

Here's something else to consider. A buttstock greatly improves your accuracy and can be used to strike the undead in hand to hand combat. Strike the skull with the full buttplate using a crushing downward blow or strike the face or back of the skull with a forward stroke holding the gun horizontally. If you try to do a vertical *(upward)* buttstroke you may break the stock at the wrist. Sporting guns with two piece stocks aren't made for that type of abuse. The pistol-grip-only shotgun is a specialty weapon in my opinion. You use it when you are defending a vehicle, or other really tight spot where you might not be able to shoulder a conventional stock.

Have a shotgun in a common gauge. That means 12 gauge *(OUCH!)* or 20 gauge *(ouch)* or .410 *(pleasant)*. I prefer 20 gauge because it still has a lot of pellets in 00 buck, I can carry more ammo and it doesn't batter the shit out of me like a 12 gauge does. I won't even bother to recover a 16 or 28 gauge gun unless there is ammo with it. We use those gauges for hunting. The 16 and 28 gauge ammo is just too hard to find.

If they aren't armed on arrival, the issue weapon to residents of Live E-town for home defense is a shotgun with ten round of ammo. You can see them drilling with them when the militias do their training on the second Sunday of the month. The gate guards and sentries patrolling the curtain wall use them too. Like I said, they don't require a lot of skill or training to use effectively and in a static position you don't have to worry so much about how much ammo you can carry.

FYI, one box of 25 rounds of 12 gauge shotgun ammo takes up about the same space as three 20 round magazines *(60 rounds total)* for an AR-15 rifle. That's a big difference. You can see why ZKs don't lug shotguns around the Dead Zone much. We're all good enough marksman that we can defend ourselves effectively with pistols in close quarters. Usually one guy on patrol will pack a shotgun to be point man if we need to enter buildings. When we go on a supply recovery run *(usually in a truck or trucks)* and know we'll need to be searching lots of buildings, you'll see a lot of shotguns in the mix. In those cases the shotguns are auxiliary weapons. When we get out of the buildings with our loot, the shotguns get stowed in the truck and we pick up our rifles again.

This is good shotgun country. Worse than high grass, thick forest with lots of brush makes the undead hard to spot.

Double barrel shotguns are not as much of a disadvantage as you might think. They are simple, don't jam and get you in the rhythm of shooting and reloading continuously quite naturally

Here a ZK instructs a new City Wall Guard in shotgun use. Most guards are armed with shotguns.

You get pretty sore after doing patrol truck duty for a while. It's also a lot harder than it looks. The moving and bouncing of the vehicle makes a shotgun a must for this work. The empty cases are returned to the armory and reloaded.

Bludgeons & Blades for Mano a Mano Zombie Combat

It is a good idea to work quietly whenever you can. Single zombies are best dealt with by just smashing in their skulls and squishing up or knocking out what remains of their brains. You can never be sure how many of them there are around and gunshots will surely attract all of them within hearing distance until some other sound or sight or smell gets their attentions. When we are on outpost duty, we don't mind attracting them so much because we're ready to take them on. When we are out patrolling and foraging the Dead Zones we usually need to be more careful. *(ex. Fire a round in a shopping mall and you'll have 1000 zombies on you in no time.)*

The best weapons to bust zombie heads depends on you. Most men have enviable brute strength that makes up for a multitude of evils. Taller guys can easily take off the top of a zombie skull by swinging a 4' piece of ¾" steel water pipe. That narrow pipe is light enough to swing quickly but heavy enough to have a lot of impact and the narrow width concentrates the impact on a small surface area. The result is the skull opens up like an eggshell and the brains usually end up a few yards away. It is a beautiful thing to behold in a Conan the Barbarian sort of way. A baseball bat, aluminum is my preference since I like the ringing sound it makes, is also a great close-in weapon. Thousands of Louisville Sluggers are doing first class work in the defense of Live E-town, the outpost line and in the Dead Zones every day. My only fear is that the wood ones sometimes break and my only complaint is that they are all a little bit bulky compared to a pipe.

If you are not so strong or so tall, you have two problems to overcome. First, you may not have the strength to deliver a bone splintering, brain splattering blow. Second, the outstretched arms of attacking zombies will often block some of your blows. They don't do this intentionally but they are so focused on eating you they just flail away at you until you kill them. This is less of a problem when you are taller than the zombies but I'm small and short so they are always plenty of limbs in my way. To overcome this I will sometimes take them out at the knees and then finish them on the ground. The other alternative is to use an edged weapon.

There were not too many real swords around prior to the apocalypse but they are being made now and some antique and replica ones are being used to good effect. Slicing swords like sabers, cutlasses, medieval swords and samurai swords are all effective. Rapiers and all sport fencing swords are pretty much useless. You need a fairly heavy blade for the kind of work we do. Fortunately there was no shortage of machetes and I've found them to be excellent if sharp. They will sever limbs that get in the way making the zombie easier to kill on the follow-up swing. Axes require more strength and accuracy but they deliver a devastating blow usually knocking aside or severing any limb that gets in the way. I knew a ZK who favored a double edged wood axe and once used it to facilitate our escape from a Walmart parking lot by wading into the undead swinging it back and forth and literally cutting a path through them. It was quite a sight. Remember, you can fight longer with a lighter machete than you can with a heavy ax.

ZKs always have plenty of big, quiet weapons handy at the outposts and on our transport when we need to travel deep into the Dead Zones. All ZKs will also have some smaller personal weapon for close combat on them at all times. Sturdy combat or survival knives, machetes and short hand axes are very common because they can do double duty as camp tools in the field and they are pretty easy to carry on your belt. A full size ax or sword or bludgeon can really get in the way and a person can only carry so much. To kill a zombie you need to destroy its brain. A hand axe *(or super-cool tomahawk)* blow will almost always slice open the skull and destroy the brain and almost never gets stuck because of its wedge shape. A strong thrust can put a knife blade through the skull most of the time but not always. Sometimes it skips off and doesn't penetrate and sometimes it penetrates and gets stuck. It's always a good idea to give it a good twist to wreck more brain tissue and hopefully break the skull bone so you can pull it out. You can drive it easily through the eye socket but I always felt that puts your hand too close to their filthy infected mouths. Some months ago I came across a vintage "knuckle duster" combat knife that has some merit. The weight of the heavy brass knuckles grip gives me enough impact to bust open skulls and I like how it protects my fingers but I'm not totally convinced of its value against zombies. It would be kick-ass for quiet work against raiders though.

I would be remiss if I did not mention the merit of simple hammers and pry bars (*crow bars*). Masonry and welding hammers are hardly different from medieval war hammers and are very effective. Big carpenter's framing hammers and ball peen hammers are also excellent skull smashers. They concentrate a lot of force on a little area and even a person of average strength can cave a skull in with one. Crowbars take a lot more strength to wield as weapons but I've found that we end up using them as crowbars more than we do as weapons when we are in the Dead Zones. They are what my father would have called a "handy item."

Let's review the basics of close combat weapons.
- The object is to cut open or crush the skull and destroy the brain by cutting into it, mashing it up inside the skull or just plain knocking it out of the skull and into the middle of next week.
- Choose something easy to carry and appropriate to your strength and height.
- Keep edged weapons sharp. *(When I say sharp, I mean shaving your bikini area sharp!)*
- When possible select hammers and hand axes where the head and handle are a single piece of steel so you never have to worry about the handle breaking.
- Tape your handle/grips with sticky tape like the golfers used back in the day so they don't slip out of your hand when they get wet *(rain, blood, pee, etc.)*
- The lighter the weapon, the longer you can fight with it before you collapse from exhaustion. *(Zombies don't get exhausted.)*
- Always clean all zombie gore off your weapons. It would suck if you got infected because you cut yourself with your own dirty weapon. *(I use car paste wax on the business end of mine so that I can clean the blades easier.)*

Here's a selection of melee weapons used by ZKs at our outpost. It's a matter of personal preference. The dead don't care what you re-kill them with.

A machete is a good choice for an apparently unaccompanied zombie.

There's nothing like a KABAR knife to really do them up. In my opinion, they are the best blades you can have for fighting, living or dead. We found a cache of these wicked beauties in a sporting good store.

"There's a zombie on the lawn," but this ZK generously took a minute away from his breakfast to quietly deal with the pest. We keep our grass in the outpost garrison area cut so any stragglers or cripplers that get in have no natural concealment.

Get away from my bike! This zombie home-owner needed quiet dispatching so we could search the property for survival critical resources. He had a broken spine so he wasn't going anywhere fast. This is an easy kill if you quickly get behind him.

General Field Gear: Staying Alive in the Dead Zone

By now you know about weapons, but there's more to staying alive in the Dead Zone than just killing zombies. I pack for the mission and missions vary. Sometimes we go in heavy with vehicles and we can bring as much as we need and leave our rucksacks on them. Other times we go in light with just what we can carry on our backs. In the basic sense, equipping for any trip into the Dead Zone is similar to a pre-apocalypse military reconnaissance mission. You are entering hostile territory when you enter the Dead Zone. There are zombies who want to eat your flesh and raiders who want to rob, rape, enslave or kill you. You need to meet all the basic requirements of survival in the field as well as keep a very low profile so you can find your enemy before they know you are there and choose the terms of engagement most advantageous to you. When you are in the Dead Zone, you are a fugitive from the law of averages. The faster you get your job done and get out, the greater your chances of survival. ZKs get jaded sometimes from too much time in the Dead Zone. I've seem good ZKs get complacent, and then careless and I've seen them get killed. I'll give you a few critical pointers that will help you get you mission done quickly and keep you alive. To get your mission done efficiently you must have the tools you will need when you need them. Otherwise you are just trusting to luck.

Protect your eyes! Get a good pair of shooting or safety glasses to protect your eyes from impact injury.   There are no eye surgeons in Live E-town. You also want to keep any zombie gore out of your eyes. Unlike you mouth, you have to keep your eyes open in the Dead Zone. Sometimes there can be a lot of blood and tissue splashing around, especially when you are fighting with clubs or blades.   You can get infected that way.

Protect your hearing. Close range gunfire, especially indoors, can leave your ears ringing enough to drive you nuts. Any ear protection is better than none. Some guys worry that they won't hear that first zombie. That may be true, but after the first round is fired next to your ear, you won't hear any of the others. The most eloquent solution to this problem is to get a set of those battery powered hearing protectors that electronically amplify all normal sounds but automatically, and instantly, ramp up the protection when loud sounds, like gunshots, are detected. Having these things on make you feel like a superhero with incredible hearing. I didn't read comic books as kid so I don't know exactly which hero that would be but trust me. These things are a must have item. Do anything that is legal, ethical and moral to obtain a pair, and a supply of batteries.

Make sure you have a light and a lot of batteries. The LED bulb lights are best because they last so long. I prefer one with a strobe feature. I think the strobe confuses the undead just like it does the living. You need light to illuminate the area and to find an escape route if things go south. You'll attract less attention to yourself without a light, but the chances of falling, getting injured on some unseen obstacle or running headlong into a zombie are just too great to risk. You should have a red filter on your light to protect your night vision and reduce the visibility of the light at a distance. Even with the red filter, throw a coat over yourself when you check a map to minimize your visibility to hostiles.

The last thing you want to do in the Dead Zone is engage zombies at night. Shots in the night will draw more when you are least able to deal with them. The undead have the advantage in the darkness. They can smell us. In the dark it's hard to use our firearms efficiently. We don't travel at night except in an emergency. We rarely camp around fires at night. Fires attract the undead and raiders. When we make fires in the Dead Zone, we make them as diversions to draw undead and raiders away from our camps. We'll keep these diversionary fires under observation in the event that survivors are drawn to them and to check on hostile activity. With no fires, we need to have extra clothing or blankets or sleep spooned up *(I get the middle!)* to stay warm enough to keep us from getting hypothermic at night. Any hot food we eat is cooked over Streno cans. If we have a tent, we'll cook inside it to warm it up before we are ready to bed down; but don't let anyone sleep inside while you do this because the fumes can kill them. It's usually better to bed down in the upper story of a defendable building that affords you good observation of the area.

You need good maps of your operations area and a compass. Getting lost increases you time in the Dead Zone and your chances of getting killed. Know where the heck you are going. Keep your maps safe and dry in plastic bags.

On a personal level, you must always be prepared for siege. You never know when you may end up separated from your team and cornered by the undead or raiders. Of the two groups, the former are more persistent but the latter are more dangerous. I've been pinned down by snipers for 10 hours and it's a lot worse than being surrounded by zombies. If you can keep the zombies out long enough, your fellow ZKs are going to try to rescue you and they will probably be successful. So just don't do anything stupid and make sure you have the following:

- **Drinking Water** - Always keep at least a canteen or bottle on you. Mix in some sugary Kool-Aid or whatever to give it some caloric value so it can serve as both food and hydration. You might even use coffee or my favorite, sweetened mangosteen herbal tea. Also have a few iodine tablets for purifying water you might find. It won't taste good but it will be safe to drink. Remember, you aren't going to last long without water. If you have no water and have the chance to grab some canned food, take the vegetables packed in water and drink that water from the can before you eat the veggies.

- **Food** - Have some on you at all times. High calorie energy bars are best for their size and weight and frankly they don't taste too much worse now than they did when they were fresh two years ago. Pack those if you can get them. If not, have a can of tuna, Spam, sardines, Vienna sausages, etc. You want a lot of calories for a small space. Candy is good too if you can tolerate it being stale. Remember, this is just to keep you alive. You don't have to like it.

- **Can-Opener** - Make sure you have the means to open a can. Don't bring a kitchen can opener. Bring one of those little military P-38 can openers or a Swiss army pocket knife. In a pinch you can use your fighting knife but it's a good way to dull the blade, spill the contents and cut yourself too.

- **Medical Kit** - Have some means to clean and dress your wounds. There's a lot of stuff to get hurt on out there. Serious cuts can get infected very quickly and I've seen a lot of people die of infections that they never would have before the world ended. Have a small vile of peroxide or alcohol, some bandage and gauze pads, a few aspirin *(but don't take these if you are bleeding)* some cotton balls or swabs and band-aids. Make sure you have a tourniquet too. You can actually survive a bite to an extremity if you can amputate it fast enough and manage to not bleed to death. You can fit all this in a space smaller than an AK-47 magazine and it hardly weighs anything.

- **Signal Mirror** - This can be a small shaving mirror or a dental mirror. It lets you signal you position to rescuers and peak around corners to see if the coast is clear without exposing yourself.

- **Firecrackers** - This is for creating a diversion to facilitate your escape. Any fireworks will do. I met a survivor who worked his way out of one mess after the other with a pack of those tiny firecrackers and a piece of rigid plastic tubing he was using as a blow gun. If the undead got him cornered, he would launch the individual lit firecrackers behind them. The undead would be drawn to the sounds behind them and he got a chance to beat feet out of there. If you use fireworks for your diversion make sure you keep them in a sealed zip-lock bag inside another sealed zip-lock bag with a lighter or matches inside so they are dry and ready when you need them. You can use your imagination on the subject of diversions. Consider the diversion value of a brick thrown through a glass window, a battery powered radio, a wind chime or a stick of dynamite. Having a few good diversions up your sleeve will save your life.

- **ZRL or Zombie Repellant Lotion** - I've heard some people jokingly refer to this as "Zombie Tan Lotion". It has nothing to do with tanning and I've always thought that joke was nonsensically stupid. You use ZRL to mask your sent in the same way hunters mask their scent from deer by splashing themselves with deer urine. You puree the most rotten zombie guts you can find *(we do it in an old Cuisinart)* and pour it into a light weight plastic bottle, preferable the squeezable kind. Then you put that in a sealed plastic bag just in case *(God forbid)* it starts to leak. It smells like a rotting corpse naturally, so we only use it when we need to remain completely un-noticed by the dead. You can imagine the scenarios. It's the kind of thing that, when needed, is desperately needed. A smart ZK makes sure to have a bottle on hand. When available on-site, fresh undead guts are preferable to ZRL. The fresh stuff is no more effective than

ZRL; but the latter is so repugnant to make, you really want to avoid having to make up a replacement bottle.

- **Swiss Army Knife or Leatherman Tool** - These little multi-purpose tools are remarkably useful. For their size, they can't be beat. I've at times carried some full size tools. A straight and Philips screwdriver can serve as weapons if need be and are useful for disassembly of things in the field. There is a queer wrench that has a swiveling head on each end, each with four different size sockets. It lets you take off or tighten nuts from ¼" to ¾". I am a girl so I don't know what this tool is called but I know it is very useful and many men have tried to trade me for it so it must be valuable.

My basic fighting load that I'll supplement with other gear as needed for the mission. I've got some small binoculars and a Brownell's tactical light in the map case too. The snacks are in case I get hungry, which I usually do.

Here's another highly versatile military set up that can be modified to match the mission by the addition or removal of pouches and pockets. The mouthpiece is for a water filled bladder carried on the back. Ammo is on his chest where he can get it fast. You must carry your gear quietly so as not to attract the undead, but how you do it is up to you. One guy has a *Hello Kitty* backpack. Suit yourself.

This ZK has a sensible load bearing vest that carries all his basic gear. It keeps his waist clear for strapping on weapons.   You'll drop your gear for freedom of movement, but you'll never drop your sidearms.

Uniform of the Live E-town ZK

Currently, there is no fixed uniform for Live E-town ZKs. I'm sure that at some time in the future there will be. For one thing, I was asked to design one. Secondly, a uniform appearance makes it easier to tell friend from foe and coveys a message of stability and authority to people you meet in the Dead Zone. That goes for raiders and survivors. I've noticed raiders show a reluctance to engage Live E-town ZKs. Survivors rescued from the Dead Zone have reported on numerous occasions that seeing everyone in a ZK group wearing the same shoulder patch is what convinced them we were not raiders and therefore safe to approach for help.

Right now, the only thing that distinguishes a ZK from anyone else in the Dead Zone or in town is the patch. Most every ZK wears it with pride on their right shoulder, possibly because it gets them perks in town like free coffee, donuts or a BJ from the truly pathetic ZK groupies.

Some outposts bought their own shirts and hats and wear unit identification patches of their own design on their left shoulders. I've never gone in for this narcissistic stuff. I know all my own people from the way they stand and I'm generally familiar with all the other ZKs at the different duty stations. I never forget a face. I've noticed a trend for all ZKs to wear pre-apocalypse military or hunting camouflage clothing. It's pretty rugged and has lots of pockets, though the older woodland camo BDU is superior in my opinion because it is longer and has hip pockets on the coat. However, keep in mind that this is from someone who has never worn it. I've never found a set small enough to fit me and when I have the time to sew, I usually find it more rewarding to play scrabble against myself.

About half of ZKs just wear rugged clothing to suit their own tastes. The colors are usually earth tones to match the terrain. You see a lot of blue denim jeans and work boots. You almost never see short sleeve shirts in the field. You see long sleeve shirts with sleeves rolled up if it is hot. ZKs know they have to protect their arms. Most zombie bites are on the arms.

My observations are that the camouflage has fundamental merit in the Dead Zone. It can confuse both the living and the dead eye. I have seen men dressed identically redirect a pack of undead. In the experiments we did, the pursued man would temporarily drop from their sight and then his identically dressed partner would present himself on their flank. All the zombies broke off their hot pursuit of the first man to chase the second, perhaps thinking that he was the first. When the two men were dressed differently, not all the zombies would break off the chase of the first man. I would recommend that any ZK uniform be camouflage if at all possible. A trip to the National Guard training areas could yield a good supply of identical uniforms in a broad range of sizes.

The Kentucky National Guardsman in our area maintain their military organization and stand ready to respond to major attacks on Live E-town but not all military units we've encountered have conducted themselves with such distinction. Probably half of the surviving organized military units went rouge when things went to hell and they are no better than raiders and a lot more dangerous. We don't need to be mistaken for them. If the ZKs go with the existing army uniform, they should have something to distinguish them from regular soldiers. One of my men suggested a white cowboy hat. Though obviously romanticizing the American fictional Lone Ranger hero, this idea has some merit. The cowboy hat is good protection from zombie and sun. I'd recommend a less visible tan or brown cowboy hat. I might even wear one myself.

Finally, fresh human blood, sweat, urine, feces and semen all attract zombies. Things that have those scents also attract zombies. When you go out in the Dead Zone, make sure you have on clean underwear. *(FYI, if Nutella chocolate spread is mixed with fresh human fluids it REALLY attracts zombies. It's the best lure I've discovered after extensive testing. I'm not sure why it works so well. There is a lot we don't know and may never know about the undead. My hypothesis is that pretty much everybody likes chocolate. In practice, this potent mixture is almost never used because most people like chocolate too much to sacrifice any amount of Nutella.)*

I sometimes see Zombie Killers wearing the ZK patch in non-regulation locations, especially in hot weather when T-shirts abound

Typical Zombie Killers in long sleeves for bite protection. The ZK shoulder patch location is correct. FYI, we don't leave our own turned.

A pair of Zombie Killers from Outpost #7 standing in front of their work. Other than their ZK patch, hardly any two will look alike at this outpost. I've seen other outposts where the officer-in-charge makes everyone dress the same. This is a logistical challenge. I think those officers that insist on it use it as a crutch for their authority. I have no need for such things.

No camo for this ZK, just comfortable neutral color outdoor clothing and a well planned load bearing rig for his patrol gear. Some ZKs like helmets, and bullet proof body armor. It's too heavy for me.

Body Armor

On a static defense line, or in a direct assault against raiders, bullet proof vests or heavy police and military body armor are great to have. In the Dead Zone, being quick on your feet is your best defense and all that armor can wear you down, dehydrate you faster, and generally reduce your effectiveness. It's not quite so bad in winter when you want extra layers and I'll occasionally use it if we are expecting trouble from raiders. Zombies don't shoot at us and they make up about 95% percent of our business these days so I don't feel like I'm at a disadvantage without a bulletproof vest. Bigger people may feel differently. One of the advantages of being small is that you are a pretty hard target to hit in the first place. In all the fighting of the last two years, I've only been shot once; and that was with a ricochet. Hitting me was pure luck on the part of the shooter and the last luck he ever had. I put a 150 grain jacketed hollow point .300 Savage through his brain. No chance of him coming back, but I digress. Getting shot hurt a lot. It nearly killed me so I don't fault anyone for armoring up. I just can't carry the weight.

The greatest threats we face are the fatal bites of the undead. A bite on a limb can be treated by the immediate severing of that limb. That's when a clean, sharp machete and a medical kit come in handy. It does open up a whole new set of problem but I've seen it done a dozen times and half of the victims survived. A bite anywhere other than a limb is always fatal if there is fluid transfer from the zombie's mouth which is the case 95 out of 100 times. All of this is pretty grim stuff but you can't dwell on it. Just prepare.

Prudent ZKs take care to protect themselves. It is actually pretty rare for us to get fatally bit. Here's how we do it. Consider that most bites are on the head, neck, shoulders, arms and hands. You hardly ever see a bite on the leg or torso. The Zombie would have to be pretty short and there are very few undead children around since most kids were consumed. You don't see bites below the arms unless you are lying down *(attacked while sleeping or crawling through high grass)* or you get overwhelmed. Those are the facts.

If you take measures to protect your head, neck, shoulders, arms and hands you will greatly increase your odds of survival. I've seen guys wear football shoulder padding and it works well but it makes it awkward to shoot a rifle. Neck-stocks like soldiers wore in the time when swords were the weapon of the day are very common now. Long hair is usually a bad idea because it gives the undead something to grab on to. I won't cut my hair. It's sort of my trademark. *(That's supposed to be me on the Live E-town seal you know.)* However, my hair is sufficiently long that I can wrap it around my neck for protection when I go in the Dead Zone. Most neck-stocks are made of leather rather than hair.

To protect your head, wear some sort of hat. Some people wear military helmets, or even fireman, motorcycle, football or construction helmets. I don't like anything that interferes with my shooting or situational awareness. The more protection a helmet offers, usually the heavier and more restrictive it is. I only use one when I know we are likely to get overwhelmed or we are going up against raiders in fixed positions. I've seen the undead drag guys down by their helmet too which is another reason I'm a little anti-helmet.

The more common headgear is a baseball hat, cowboy hat or some type of visored hunting hat or military hat *(with the exception of that stupid black beret)*. They serve a practical purpose as well as a protective one. The wide, stiff brimmed cowboy hats offer good protection because they let you know when a zombie is coming in to bite. The zombie's face will hit the brim before his teeth hit your neck or ear giving you a split second to take evasive action. The cowboy hat has saved a lot of lives. A zombie has a hard time sinking his teeth into a broad surface like your skull so any hat is usually going to protect you from that first bite and buy you some reaction time.

When the weather is right for it, most of us will wear heavy leather coats for the excellent protection they offer. Likewise, gloves are the norm. It's hard to have good trigger control with bulky gloves so most ZK will search far and wide for a pair that fits them well or take them off it they have to shoot.

In the hot months, any extra gear or protective clothing is a real drag on patrol. The solution I've found to work most effectively is to apply light armor to my Dead Zone clothing. Remember, we are trying to stop bites, not bullets. The heavy plastic that laundry detergent bottles used to be made out of is excellent armor. Try biting through it and you'll see what I mean. There are a few businesses in Live E-town that will apply this plastic armor to the garments of your choice for a moderate fee. Some ZKs do it themselves. Sewing is not one of my best skills. *(I was never very good at suturing.)* I have my plastic armor made. Styles vary, but usually there is a forearm and an upper arm guard at the very least. Sometimes the shoulders and elbows are done too. Sometimes it is glued, stapled or sewn to the outside. Sometimes it is exposed and sometimes it is covered in matching cloth so it blends into the garment. If we are the knights of the post apocalyptic world, recycled plastic is our armor. Oh, how the mighty have fallen.

Transportation

Road travel in the Dead Zone is complicated by the large numbers of wrecked and abandoned cars on the main arteries. At this stage, the roads themselves are still in decent shape but nature is encroaching on them. The grass grows unchecked and obstructs your view of the roadside and the plant life has taken root on the roadway itself where leaves and soil have been blown up against vehicles and other obstacles. The roads have lots of places for the undead to be concealed and they are there in numbers. They are belted into their cars, crawling around crippled from the crashes that killed them, and I've even seen them walking on the roadside with gas cans in their hand. Roadways are great places to get bitten.

As we pushed out the perimeter of Live E-town we completely cleared the roads and used the car bodies in our defensive works. Outside the perimeter we have moved the cars to the side of the road. Where there were enough of them, we formed them into a continuous wall, like parked cars on a city street. Make and model of each car, general condition, and location are recorded in case we ever need it as a spare parts source. We bring back the most useful vehicles for the Live E-town motor pool. Those are four-wheel-drive trucks and cars, large tractor trailers *(fuel tankers especially)* and smaller rear wheel drive trucks from pick-ups to multi-axles. These are all important for supply recovery work in the Dead Zone and to a lesser degree, transportation of equipment and people in town. For police, medical and government use in town, we've assembled quite a fleet of small, super fuel efficient cars.

Out in the Dead Zone, I want a four-wheel-drive SUV or a pick-up, preferably with a winch and definitely with a tow hitch for a trailer. Two-wheel-drive cars and trucks are easy to get stuck if you go off the hard road surface. Four-wheel-drive gets us most anywhere we need to go. Tactically it gives us a great advantage in that we can quickly maneuver around Raiders on foot or in road-bound two-wheel-drive vehicles. Four-wheel-drive gets us around or over the undead as necessary.

We make some modifications to our Dead Zone vehicles to adapt them to the environment. The glass is protected by expanded metal mesh which is attached by bolts, welding or both. I prefer both. The undead can't get in and you can still shoot out the window if you want to. Modified like this, enclosed SUVs or pick-up trucks with a cap are very good temporary shelters in the Dead Zone. You can sleep in one if you have too, or wait out rescue if you get overrun. In a jam, you can take shelter in any car. It's better than getting eaten, but at best it will only delay your death unless you are rescued. If the undead see you there, they will surround you and they won't go away unless they are distracted by something else to eat or you die of dehydration and reanimate yourself.

On the outside of our vehicles we add racks for carrying extra gasoline, spare tires and equipment for the mission *(personal gear and food we keep inside)*. Front and rear bumpers are reinforced for pushing *(moving abandoned cars and obstacles)* and the headlights and radiator are protected from damage with heavy metal grills. Sometimes trucks have a ram installed on the front that is shaped like a shallow "V" to part the undead and push them aside. Hit them fast enough and you'll cripple or kill them of course. This modification is good if you have to smash through a half-assed road block too, but don't try that with anything substantial.

Some, but not all of our vehicles, have roof hatches and floor hatches added to them. Both can be used for escape. The roof hatch is usually open when we patrol. We get better situational awareness when we have a ZK up there. He'll use binoculars to check the way ahead.

Live E-town motor pool doesn't bother armoring our vehicles much anymore since raiders generally avoid us now. Armor adds a lot more weight and that cuts back on gas mileage and reduces our patrol range. We still keep helmets and bullet proof vests in the truck since we are the most vulnerable to incoming fire when we are in the vehicle. Some ZK wear them. I don't.

We always have at least one substantial radio on any vehicular patrol in the Dead Zone so we can communicate with ZKs in the field or the base station at Live E-town. Standard operating procedure is to leave one ZK at the truck to monitor the radio.

All vehicles will have some kind of spotlight for night work, weapon racks to secure longarms safely inside, a siren to distract the undead, and a no-key ignition system when possible. On older vehicles they just remove the lock from the column so anyone can start it without a key. This has proven very handy and reduces the number of keys needed by half.

In the Dead Zone we hardly ever use motorcycles for patrol because they are too loud and you spend too much time navigating the debris field all around you so you don't crash. Nobody on a motorcycle can effectively watch for the undead or raiders in that situation. We use motorcycles for distracting and drawing off the undead when a lot of noise is desirable.

Bicycles and horses are used occasionally in the Dead Zone for certain missions. The problem with both of these forms of transportation is that they leave you exposed and vulnerable to the undead, they require a lot of your focus to manage safely, they are difficult to fight from and they don't allow you much additional carrying capacity if you find survivors or supplies. That being said, they require no gasoline, are pretty quiet and horses and mountain bikes can traverse some pretty rugged terrain. It takes a special kind of reconnaissance ZK to use them effectively. Long, strong legs help too.

Nobody is refining any fuel anymore so gasoline is a precious commodity and its recovery continues to be a high priority mission. Likewise for LP gas. My team has siphoned the fuel from thousands of cars in the last year and a half. We could build a pyramid like the ones in Egypt with all the red plastic gas cans and LP tanks we've found in garages. Once a car or residence is checked for fuel it's marked with a "G" on the windshield or front door. You won't find a drop of fuel in cars or lawn mowers or barbeque grills in the Dead Zone within ten miles of the perimeter. Live E-town has it all stored in the underground tanks of gas stations and on the surface in salvaged 55 gallon drums and other containers in various well guarded fuel dumps. Inside the walls people have what they have but it is costly to get more.

Horses, wagons and carriages have made a comeback in the 21st century. It's rare to see a car driving around in Live E-town anymore except for the people movers and buses. The schedules they run aren't like the ones you'd find before the apocalypse. They go where they need to go and when they need to go and no more. The expression "You missed the bus," implies a serious and consequential mistake on your part. Precautions are taken to see that this doesn't happen. Usually the drivers have a passenger list that they check to make sure they have everybody they came with. The good news is that if you do really miss the bus, if you can find people they are likely to shelter you for the night.

Around Live E-town you still see a lot of cars in driveways and garages, but they aren't driven much, if at all. People like to sit in

them and kids play in them. Families even wash them sometimes.
It's like they are monuments to our lost civilization and people cling
to them in hope of its return. If you see somebody driving a car in
town, it's likely to be police or emergency response.

You can actually buy a little fuel for the purposes of maintaining
a vehicle you have. The Mayoral Council sees operational vehicles
as a good thing. Some people have converted their vehicles to
alternative fuels like ethanol or bio-diesel or LP gas. They don't
drive far with very few exceptions. I know of several people who
left the city in search of lost loved ones. Very few have returned.
It makes more sense to hire a ZK to do that kind of thing for you.

Car accidents were a leading cause of injury and death in the U.S.
before the apocalypse. Now it's bicycle, horseback riding and
motorcycle accidents. Bicycles are by far the most common
individual transportation inside the city walls. They don't have to
be fed or groomed and don't crap all over the place like horses. If
you don't have to go too far, and the area you travel in is secure,
bicycles are great.

Motorcycles are permitted but they need to have good quiet
mufflers on them. Since gas is so costly, those that have
motorcycles will keep them in the garage for emergencies. You
wouldn't see someone casually going on a cruise around town or
even commuting to their job on one. If you spot someone in town
on a motorcycle, it is usually a Live E-town mailman.

One final note on driving in the Dead Zone or Live E-town. If
you hit a zombie, please kill it. Plowing into them usually just
cripples them and they end up crawling into the high grass where
it's hard to locate them. People get killed trying to flush out
crippled zombies. I'm not trying to discourage you from hitting
them, just make sure you finish the job. All you need to do is back
over their head and that's that. Make sure you let the motor pool
people know you did this so they can clean the gore off the vehicle
so nobody gets accidentally infected from it when they are working
on or under the vehicle.

Here's ZK patrol truck #17 from Outpost #7 with its crew. They like to play ice cream truck music when driving around to call the undead out.

Interior of the patrol truck fighting compartment from above. Lots of Molotov cocktails and zombie blood on the walls.

Ammo racks keep your shells organized and handy for fast reloads.

ZK patrol truck gunners "do it on the roll." That's their motto.

Survivor Rescue

Human beings have an incredible capacity for survival. Even two years into this living hell we still find survivors. People, individually and in small groups, have been hunkered down in secure enclaves since this mess started. I think that initially your survival depended a lot on luck. This infection hit so fast it didn't give people enough time to intellectually process what was going on. One day we were hearing about huge violent riots in Louisville and two days later our friends and neighbors were eating each other. There weren't many official announcements. I never heard anything on a national level from the Center for Disease Control (CDC) or the military. Local radio WQXE got the true facts on the air but it was fairly late in the game. They were the first to get civil authorities to confirm that a bite was sure death. Official confirmation of the threat early on would have gotten people doing the things they needed to and saved a lot of lives, but who the hell saw this shit coming? Looking back on it, most local, state and federal government agencies fell apart (military fared the best) and the new leaders that emerged where the ones like Mayor Max White, who had the presence of mind to see beyond their own loss and fear, figure out what was going on, and take appropriate action. It's because of Max White that Live E-town has a ZK force and survivor rescue remains a top priority. He is one of a handful of people that I actually like, and I'm not saying that because he's paying me to write this.

Every day ZKs patrol the Dead Zones for survivors. There isn't a town or farm or wood in a thirty mile radius that we haven't swept on foot or at least from the air. Searching for survivors is about maintaining hope. When we put planes up, we fly them on the same course for three days in a row. That gives survivors time to spot our pilots and send up a signal. The undead can't fly planes. When survivors hear a plane, they know someone is alive somewhere. They'll almost always find a way to signal us. *(Raiders will run for cover.)* Once we know where they are, we'll walk or drive out there to make contact with them immediately. We've got to find them before their luck runs out. We never communicate survivor locations by radio in the clear. It's either in code or by runner after the planes return. Runner is safer. You never know who is listening on your frequency and making contact with survivors is dangerous enough without having to fight through a raider ambush too. Once we get the facts we move out fast. Any number of things could cause the survivors to move from their reported location, and as I said before, to maximize your own odds for survival you want to minimize your time in the Dead Zone.

When we patrol the Dead Zone we leave our tags painted on Walmarts, K-marts, Target stores, pharmacies, water towers, grocery stores, police stations, and gun shops along the paths survivors are likely to take. These are the places survivors go to get the things they need to survive. Along with those tags we'll leave dated messages, listing our safe house locations, radio stations we monitor, and our next patrol date. Survivors see these tags and hopefully our recent messages and it gives them hope that someone is out there ready to help them. We've brought in over 3,500 survivors from the safe house program in just the last six months. It's not without its problems. Raiders are also looking for survivors for their own purposes, mostly as slaves, concubines, gladiators and in some rare cases food. We never hold to the advertised patrol schedule to keep the raiders guessing. We'll check our safe houses once a week or more if they are close.

A safe house is just that. We select a solid defendable structure and secure it against the undead, and to the extent we can, raiders. Brick or concrete block buildings are the best because they don't burn easily and the walls are strong enough to keep the undead out. Even better if they have some kind of wall or fence around the perimeter. If they don't, we'll ring them with cars to form a makeshift perimeter wall. A living human in a hurry can get over a parked car in a second but to a zombie it's like one of those rock wall climbs you used to see at county fairs. It slows them down big time if they are chasing you and keeps them from messing up the yard when nobody is around. *(Zombies do poop you know. They poop out the undigested rotting flesh they've eaten as they fill up their GI tract. It's disgusting to step on in bare feet.)*

To prepare a safe house we'll heavily board up all the downstairs, zombie accessible, windows, reinforce the doors and add crossbars to lock them from the inside, stock the place with a small supply of food, water, blankets, first aid kit, candles, matches, and hand weapons. *(At some safe houses we bury firearms, ammo and radio equipment for our own use in an emergency.)* We also clean the place up and provide clean beds. In the Dead Zone, a safe place to sleep is what you want, and a safe clean place to sleep with a little food and water is a miracle. Miracles give survivors hope and hope keeps them going. We even set out some five gallon buckets with toilet seats and plastic bags for sanitation along with a little reading material on Live E-town and maps of the area showing locations of other safe houses. All the comforts of home with the key under the welcome mat. Plenty of times I've seen ambitious survivors work their way right up to the outpost line by following the safe house maps.

If a survivor can make it to the safe house, they can essentially hold up in there until the cavalry arrives. The well organized raiders groups don't bother with them too much anymore because they know we're coming and they don't want to get caught in the act of attacking or plundering Live E-town property. On those occasions that we've interrupted a raider siege of our safe houses or caught them trying to ambush survivors on the way there, we kill them all and set their heads on pikes. It's kind of medieval but we don't have much trouble with them anymore so I guess it works.   When they see the undead eyes of their raider buddies looking back and forth it really gives them the heebie-jeebies. We aren't so brutal when it's a matter of conflicts over resources, but the ZKs take their survivor rescue mission very seriously.

We use those safe houses ourselves operationally when we are doing long patrols in the Dead Zones. The farthest safe houses we have are 50 miles out. We've brought in survivors from Dead Lexington at those.

Unfortunately, not all the survivors are worth saving. Life in the Dead Zone for any length of time can do a lot of psychological damage. You develop major trust issues to say the least. The infected obviously don't go back to Live E-town. Neither do perverts, violent criminals, or the dangerously insane. A ZK makes a lot of judgment calls in the Dead Zone. If a survivor of questionable sanity has the sense to go to a safe house, there's usually some hope of returning them to a functional degree of mental stability. We'll leave that to the doctors. When we find a survivor in the open that's bat-shit-crazy and reminds us of the Gollum character from Lord of the Rings, you can bet they are too dangerous to bring in. We won't endanger the community or our team. Sometimes we'll leave the Gollum to the Dead Zone, sometimes we have to kill them so they don't kill us. We always kill convenience cannibals and kid-touchers and I'll kill rapists but a lot of the other ZKs will let that slide if the person has skills. Recently they've asked us to bring the undesirables to the hospital. I hope it's for vaccine experiments. Just to be safe, I cripple them first.

On a personal level, for me the mission of survivor rescue comes behind killing zombies. But, it is so close behind it can smell zombie killing's shampoo. I want to protect people and I especially want to protect children, because it is the right thing to do. The reason I have to put zombie killing first is four days into this apocalypse Msgr. Bohlin, the Vicar of the Prelature of Opus Dei in New York City, called me and told me to do it. *(Yes, it's true. I'm not from around here.)* The Prelate's take on it was the zombies were Satan's imps and had to be destroyed at all costs. He said the numeraries were arming themselves to take the field against the abomination, and I should do the same. So technically, I have to put zombie killing first if I'm going to stay on the right side of God. Doing God's work makes me feel good inside. Saving children makes me feel even better. I can't help it. I love little kids.

A ZK looking for the living in an overrun survivor campsite in the Dead Zone. People can survive by staying quiet and still in closed tents. Zombie often won't look inside if they don't hear or see anything.

Here's a muddle of survivors and undead to sort out! Survivor, zombie, zombie, survivor, zombie, zombie. If you can shoot that in less time than it takes to say it, you should be a contract zombie killer.

A well stocked ZK safe house in the Dead Zone.

Rescuing survivors is the most rewarding part of the job. Others like the money, or the perks, or the excitement, or the chance for revenge.

Diversion

As much as I'm sure you want to, we can't go out and attack every herd of zombies we find in the Dead Zone. If we are going to win this war, we need to bide our time, engage the enemy only on the terms and ground of our choosing and most importantly, avoid contact with overwhelming numbers of the undead. We've tried fighting them toe to toe (*Rorke's Drift style*) before and we came very close to being overrun. It was air power, fire bombing, bulldozers and some incredible sacrifices that stemmed the tide of undead that was rising over us and won those early battles.   The undead are a tough adversary. We know that they don't get tired. They don't get scared away. They don't retreat. Wounds don't deter them. Thank goodness they are relatively easily distracted.

Another major aspect of our work as ZKs is preventing large herds of undead from attacking Live E-town. The way we do that is to first find those herds. Then we get them walking away from our fair city, preferably into a raider encampment or, if we have the resources to exterminate them, into one of our prepared traps. Like much of what we do, this is risky work.

Air reconnaissance spots 60% of the herds and ground patrols the remainder. Anything spotted by ground will usually be investigated from the air since dense concentrations of undead in the area make it hard for ground patrols to operate. The information gathered from the ZKs in the air will be used to plot the herd's path on the terrain map and determine if and where it should be diverted. Sometimes we can easily get them channeled right into a killing zone and burn them up or crush them. Other times there are so many that we black out the city and perimeter and enforce total silence while ZKs get into position to distract the herd.

The actual work of diversion is done by several teams of ZKs operating dirt racing motorcycles. We usually transport the cyclist in the back of 6x6 all-wheel drive, five-ton army trucks with quiet commercial mufflers installed. We get on the side of the herd, the side we want to turn them to, and let the cyclist loose. They ride into the perimeter of the herd like cowboys, whooping and yelling until they see it is starting to come toward them. Then they become Pied Pipers. Our air recon plane will confirm the herd's direction change by radio.

It gets very dangerous for the cyclist because in addition to attracting the herd, they are attracting all the undead in the area who begin to converge on them from all sides. Even though the unwanted undead followers are considerably fewer in number, they have a habit of popping out in your way at the most inopportune times. To protect the Pied Pipers, a second group of cyclist and four-wheelers will take point and try to clear the path. Their shooting helps to get the attention of the herd and keep them shuffling in the desired direction.

When the herd is safely redirected, we'll stand the teams down. In the day time this entails having them race ahead and disappear over the horizon, closest knob or whatever offers them concealment. If the diversion work runs into the night, it isn't always possible to get the team out of the field. It's too dangerous to race ahead blindly into the Dead Zone without headlights. In that scenario the team will head for a safe house to hunker down in total silence and darkness hoping the undead herd will pass them by unnoticed.

Very large herds can be difficult to turn. You can draw off chunks of them from the sides but the main body will frequently keep plodding along unaware that those on the side have even left. We've had success changing the direction of really large herds (1000+) by buzzing them at very low altitude. It works best if you make a single pass down the middle, from one side of the herd to the other, and hold the course until they are out of sight behind you. If they see the plane bank and turn around, they will sometimes track the direction change and you don't want that. The low buzz definitely gets their attention. The best pilots go so low we have to clean the brains off the landing gear when they get back to Addington Field. As you might guess, aircraft have first priority on gasoline and aircraft parts are Survival Critical Resources (SCR) on supply missions. Those light planes, and their pilots and observers, are Live E-town's early warning system.

We mostly use motorcycles for diversion work but this dune buggy (nick named the "Doom Buggy") has turned out to be useful as a fast gun platform. The machine gun is loaded with blanks to get the attention of the undead.

Raider Control

The Dead Zones are called that for a reason. Most of the inhabitants are undead. There are a few scattered small settlements, mostly family farms, and we continuously find survivors *(individuals and small groups)* trying to stay alive day to day. As if things weren't hard enough already, there are about 25 organized raider groups operating in the Dead Zones too. Raiders prey on other survivors. Raider is a catch all term for any living person or group of people regularly involved in crimes directed against another living person in the Dead Zone.

Now, it's no crime to take gas out of an abandoned car, or to break into an abandoned house and take food, clothes or whatever. One might even argue convincingly that survivors struggling to stay alive in the Dead Zone have a natural right of self preservation. In the Dead Zone, it is kill or be killed. If you can kill another person for their food or ammo and stay alive another day, that's what Darwin would call "survival of the fittest." To stay alive in a barbarous world, human beings can descend to the level of animals with frightening ease. The difference is the raiders like it. Before the apocalypse they were animals disguised as people. When civilization fell away, there was nothing to keep them in check. Raiders just get off on robbery, kidnapping, rape, torture, murder and enslavement. With a few notable exceptions, raiders are sociopathic scumbags. That's probably why they survived.

Live E-town and its ZKs regard most raider groups as hostile threats and act accordingly. You almost can't go wrong killing them in our patrol area. The fact is the motivation of the different raider groups vary. If you know those motivations, you can use it to do your job more efficiently. For the sake of brevity I will discuss only four groups, one from each patrol region.

Lords of Hell

The Lords of Hell seem to be homicidal maniacs who just enjoy killing *(living and undead)*. They use a lot of motorcycles and adorn them with active *(but toothless)* zombie heads. The ones we have captured tell us they are Satan's angles chosen to punish the sinners left behind by the rapture, more or less. We have observed them to practice necrophilia. They are bat-shit-crazy and very dangerous. They are one of the few raider groups that will attack ZK patrols. In fact, they have even attacked the outpost line. Fortunately there are probably less than 100 of them. They move from place to place in the Dead Zone, drawing the undead into specially prepared killing fields with the noise of their motorcycles and then systematically decapitating them with orgiastic delight. Any living survivor captured by them will be tortured, frequently by mutilation and dismemberment, and often consumed alive. It's a good day when I get to send one of these freaks to meet their boss.

Cavers

The Cavers are basically highwaymen that attempt to control passage along 31W and 31E where they are closest together between Dead Horse Cave and Dead Munfordville. They have a lookout post on top of Dawson's Knob where they watch for survivor traffic on both roads and Interstate 65. Dawson's Knob is right in the middle of that road net no more than three miles from either extreme and half a mile from 31W. Most survivors, if they've lived this long, know to stay off the major highways like I-65 because they are the paths of least resistance for the undead. Route 31W and 31E are much safer paths of travel.

The leader of the Cavers is a man named James Redmon. Rumor has it that he was a hardened career criminal before the apocalypse who spent as much of his life in prison as he did out. Whatever the truth of it is, he has a group of about 150 followers, and holds perhaps as many again as slaves. Redmon's motivation is the survival of his gang and he's very conservative in his actions.

Somehow, Redmon got control of Mammoth Cave which he uses as a secure enclave for his operations and storage for his supplies. The slaves are employed in agricultural work growing food and tending livestock for the Cavers so they don't have to go foraging too deeply into the Dead Zone towns. In fact, the Caver gang members spend most of their time avoiding the undead. The national park had few residents and the rugged terrain keeps the wandering undead in the valleys where they are easy to spot and block. Redmon planned to lay low until all this blew over and he choose a good spot to do it. However, being holed up like that, he ran short of supplies early on and turned to banditry and then slavery. Now his goal is self-sufficiency for the long term.

Caver scouts watch the roads in that seven mile wide corridor and alert their well armed ambush teams by radio if they spot survivors . Those ambush teams intercept the survivors and try to convince them to come with them to safety. Thinking this is the answer to their prayers, most survivors fall for it. In that case, the able bodied men, women and children are usually pressed into slavery unless their freedom can be purchased with food, ammunition or some other commodity. The sick will usually not make it back to the cave. They'll get separated from their fellow travelers and be discretely executed. Redmon doesn't want any useless mouths.

If the survivors refuse to go and put up a fight, they might get away. Redmon is after the easy targets and isn't willing to commit his people and limited resources to difficult endeavors. His ambush parties rarely even pursue combative survivors. Fighters don't make good slaves after all. Likewise, he usually doesn't pursue escaped slaves vigorously. The dangers of tracking them down in the Dead Zone aren't worth it to him. We have rescued nine of these escapes.

From what we know, Redmon acts in the manner of a feudal king and treats his slaves comparatively well. They are compelled to hard work but they are protected, fed from their labors, and although they might be whipped for disobedience, they are not tortured, nor are they sexually violated as a matter of practice. Sometimes slaves even come into the gang fold through what passes for marriage these days or by earning the trust and friendship of a gang member. The other thing of note about Redmon is that he does not harm children. When families are captured, children are allowed to stay with their parents and orphaned children are adopted and cared for by the gang members' families. There is something in him that recognizes that his future, and that of the human race, depends on children.

The Caver ambush teams made the mistake of attacking ZK patrols a few times. The first two occasions we counter-attacked, killed them all, and then killed the observers on Dawson's Knob. The third time they attacked us we let some run to get word back to Redmon. Since then we pass unmolested. Our patrols put lots of warning signs up south of the Cavers to redirect northbound survivors away from 31W and 31E. I'll bet you Redmon still doesn't know they are there. We know the signs are working because the survivors are getting to Live E-town.

It is currently not in Live E-town's interest to attack the Cavers.

It might be someday. For now, Redmon is at least keeping a fairly large group of people alive. It seems as likely as not that his slaves will ultimately revolt and overthrow him. Half of his population are slaves which he does not appear to treat harshly enough to crush their spirits nor kindly enough to win their loyalty.

Bardstown Ballers (BBs)

On supply runs into Boston, Cravens, Bellwood, and Bardstown itself, I've had contact with a typically vicious, moderate sized group of approximately thirty raiders who call themselves the Bardstown Ballers. Their present leader is a 25 year old man called Donny Smith. He is the oldest member of his group. Average age is probably 20 years old and 30% of the members are girls. The Ballers (or BBs) devote themselves to the pursuit of what pleasures the derelict world has to offer with their main focus on drugs and sex. They cook up their own meth and grow their own marijuana. We have found their crops on occasion. My men keep these crops under close observation so they can ambush the BBs at harvest time, or so they say. We have killed several BBs over the past two years in pharmacies in conflicts over prescription medicines, mostly painkillers and stimulants. We killed their previous leader and a third of their gang last summer when we caught them laying siege to one of our safe houses off Route 62. Now they steer clear of ZK patrols.

If I get good intelligence on their movements, I'll act on it with extreme prejudice. Like a lot of raiders, the Bardstown Ballers have no fixed base and move from place to place in the Dead Zone until the resources are exhausted or the undead drive them out. Their idea of a good time is to capture survivors and hold them prisoner so they can be raped repeatedly. If there is no hope of ransom, they will murder their captives once they become bored with them. We know they have traded captives to other raider groups for use in spectator zombie vs. human death matches. From information gleaned in our patrols, I estimate the BBs have raped and murdered approximately 50 men, women and children. They are sadists and perverts and we will kill them on sight in the Dead Zone. They can't be rehabilitated because there is nothing there to rehabilitate. They were always rabid animals but civilization kept them in check. You can't let rabid animals roam freely biting people.

General's Tribe of the Ohio (GTO)

This group of riverine raiders control the Ohio River from McAlpine Dam to Dead Cincinnati, most of the bridges over it and the fortified towns of Live Westport (est. population 350) and Live Milton (est. population 3500) which they established. Their leader is a charismatic 31 year old former prison guard named Brad LeGrange, commonly known as General Motors. His deputy and enforcer is a former union pipe-fitter called Chief Kick-Ass. *(General Motors dresses like a Napoleonic general in a blue tailcoat with gold epaulets and gold braid decoration, and a big plumed hat with a cockade made of the chrome trim "GTO" letters from an old Pontiac. He carries a sword. Chief Kick-Ass wears what I'm told is a genuine American Indian chief's long, feathered headdress which was looted from the Frazier Museum. Chief Kick-Ass is an expert marksman and always armed with a scoped MAK 90. He decorated the wooden stock with upholstery tacks like a wild west Indian probably would have if they had AK-47s in the old West.)*

My qualified guess is that GTO has 375 working members on its boats, bridge outposts, and Dead Zone riverside bases. It's hard to pin down the number of raiders in this group because General Motors seems to be able to draw draftees as needed from Live Westport and Live Milton. He is highly regarded as a savior and protector in these survivor communities. He is unquestionably a pirate, kidnapper and thief, but these days that doesn't necessarily make you a bad person. To Live Milton and Live Westport, he is a beloved benefactor. Judging from my experiences with General Motors, I would say he is one of the few raiders that probably isn't a sociopath. I believe his actions in the first weeks of the apocalypse are demonstrative of his true personality.

On the forth day of the apocalypse he fought his way out of the prison where he was employed. He brought with him a group of followers including 14 guards and 57 prisoners. The latter he personally selected and issued weapons from the prison armory. His objective was to seize both the Belle of Louisville and the Spirit of Jeffersonville riverboats. He did so and impressed their crews at gunpoint. Under his command these boats were operated continuously, night and day, for the next week evacuating survivors from Louisville until it was consumed in a firestorm from incendiary bombing. Later he would lead these survivors in retaking and fortifying the small towns of Westport and Milton to establish secure enclaves.

You will note that General Motors' area of operations is outside my patrol responsibility. I had occasion to deal with him as an emissary for Live E-town on several occasions. Physically he is not striking. He is perhaps 5'9" tall and somewhat overweight. He wears thick glasses and sports outlandish sideburns. In fact, his whole demeanor is outlandish but with a disarming and very entertaining dry humor. He is also ruthless with his enemies and merciless to traitors. I saw him summarily execute a servant who was caught stealing one of his personal rifles. He said to the man, "Steve Reyling, you have betrayed me. It pains me to do this, but I cannot have a man on my crew who I cannot trust." At that point, he politely asked if I could wait a few minutes while he dealt with this unfortunate internal matter. He then had the man pulled to the deck and held on his back. He looked around him and picked up a little 2 ounce tack hammer and a 10" piece of rebar that were nearby. He hammered the rebar through the thief's eye socket and into his brain. The man screamed in agony for the entire 10 minutes it took to kill him. It took that long because the hammer was so little and it required dozens of strokes to drive the thick blunt bar in. Everyone watched in silence. I must say, even if this was staged for my benefit, I was favorably impressed with the General's grasp of the leadership value of judiciously applied cruelty. Men fear torture and death far more than death alone.

General Motors' motivation seems to be two-fold. First is the aggressive pursuit of a debauched, hedonistic lifestyle for himself. *(For example, he has seven "wives" two of whom were unashamedly felating him during our last formal diplomatic meeting on his riverboat.)* Second, he seems genuinely interested in the welfare of his pirate crew and the citizens of Live Milton and Westport. (For example, I'd estimate 95% of the booty he recovers from one means or another goes to the survivors in the towns. His pirates and people will tell you as much.)

General Motors holds his gang to a very strict standard of conduct which reminds me of pre-apocalypse organized crime. You can count on them to act in a professional and businesslike manner. They have always been true to their word in every encounter we have had with them. If you need to move something down from

Dead Cincinnati, the General is the man to see. We have a treaty in place with the GTO and share intelligence on zombie movements as well as trade with them for certain supplies and human capital. My last encounter with the General centered on the trade of the Lincoln convertible limousine President John F. Kennedy was assassinated in for two civil engineers and a Merck chemist. I understand the General, Chief Kick Ass and some of their wives like to go tooling around crippling zombies in it.

I could write more on these raider groups and I probably will. This should give you an idea of what you are getting into when you sign up to be a ZK. Maybe you see something here you like better than being a ZK. If that's the case; have at it, but keep in that I concur with General Motors regarding disloyalty.

Save the full-auto for raiders. It's wasted on the undead. This ancient light machine gun has served us pretty well. It is very effective against vehicles.

Supply Acquisition

Just as the shock of living through the apocalypse was starting to wear off, there was the additional shock of realizing how fast we were running out of the material things we thought we needed to live. As a woman, I think I can speak for my gender as a whole, the loss of toilet paper seemed like a fatal blow. Much to my surprise, toilet paper was not a survival critical resource. I still think it is a civilization critical resource, but the fact is you don't die without it. There are a lot of things you will die without, and it's our job as ZKs to facilitate the location, collection and recovery of survival critical resources (SCR).

Some SCRs are: weapons, ammunition and ammo reloading equipment and components, food, medicine, medical & first aid equipment & supplies, aircraft parts, livestock, horses, farming equipment, seed, fertilizer, pesticides, light bulbs, fuel *(gasoline, diesel, LP gas, kerosene)*, generators, pumps, sanitation equipment and chemicals, matches, batteries, and communication equipment. There were a lot of resources within the Live E-town perimeter to get us going. We were fortunate to have a hospital, fire equipment, radio station, and a wide range of manufacturing businesses and heavy construction and earth moving equipment. A lot of the important, impossible to acquire stuff was already here. Keeping it going is the challenge.

On our patrols, we systematically search the area for supplies. Obviously we can only carry so much. What we don't take back we make note of so we can get it later. If we are on foot, we fill our pockets and packs. If we have a vehicle and trailer, we'll fill it to cargo capacity. Once we've located a large cache or a particularly SCR rich area, we'll escort a civilian recovery team to the site and protect them while they load it into their tractor trailers. This is the most efficient way to do this work. We got truck loads from military armories and big box stores early on that were essential to our survival.

The undead and raiders interfere with our SCR recovery efforts. An area with a lot of dead often has a lot of SCR in the cupboards and closets and garages of private homes and on the shelves of its businesses. Make no mistake, this is dangerous and tedious work. It takes care and attention to detail. You just don't yank open doors unless you're looking to have undead children biting off your junk.

A large number of kids died in their homes. This is no time to get sentimental either. Just clear the undead first and then give it a look over. You check the kitchen and pantry for canned or dry food. Check the top of the fridge, closets and any office desks or bedrooms *(underneath and between mattress & box spring)* for guns and ammo. Check the bathroom and bedrooms for medicines and first aid stuff. Check the garage and sheds for fuel, useful tools, radios, etc.

When you are clearing a house, it's easier with a two man team but it can be, and regularly is, done solo. Some ZKs prefer that so they don't have to worry about a big mouth partner giving away their presence or distracting them with woody banter. Either way, you have to be quiet and listen. The undead may detect you by your scent before you detect them. They'll start to move around to get to you and if you are quiet you will probably hear them. When they see you they'll begin that hellish moaning which you need to put a stop to immediately before they call every damn zombie in earshot down on you.

Clearing houses is where a silenced pistol comes in handy but it's usually not the end of the world if you have to fire an un-silenced gun indoors. Houses tend to contain the noise of gunshots, especially if the windows are intact, so they may not be noticed by anybody other than the closest undead. I close the front door behind me to keep the sound in and too keep any undead from walking in behind me. *(Make sure you check the peep hole before you walk out that door again.)*

I use a big claw framing hammer to open cabinets and I'm especially careful of doors that open in. Most of the time I'll just unlatch them and then kick them in or push them open with a hammer. Rooms in a house are so small you aren't going to have much luck surprising any undead indoors. They could be right on the other side of the door, under the bed, on the floor of the closet, in the vanity, sitting in chair at a desk, or whatever. You name it; I've seen it. You need to be on your game, safety off, hammer, hatchet , machete or whatever in your off hand, and totally focused to quickly identify and eliminate your target. It's close range and you don't have a lot of reaction time.

I don't know why it is, but a good portion of the undead seem to have stayed put. When we are indoors we often find them where they died two years ago. Try to read the scene when you enter a

residence or building. Look for dried blood on the floors and walls.
It you see a lot of blood on a door it means that something dead was
trying to get at something alive on the other side at one time.
Whoever that was may have escaped or may be dead in there now.

There is usually no SCR in attics but there are sometimes undead
up there. This is something to be on the alert for lest they come
crashing down on you through the ceiling. This is kind of funny
when you see it unless it happens to you. Being quiet helps avoid
disturbing the zombies in the attic. I recommend pulling out of a
house were you hear movement in the attic. You are at a real
disadvantage if you try to go after them in tight spaces like that,
especially if the access is via a closet crawlspace or drop down
ladder. Just get out of there before one of the damn things falls on
you. You can safely kill it later by burning the whole house down.

Basements often have SCR. We find a lot of ammo, reloading
equipment and ammunition components, radios and canned food in
basements. They are a bit more popular with the undead than attics
but they can be easier to deal with. With the cellar, you have the
advantage of height over the undead and they usually collect in the
stairwell for you. Remember you can usually hear people walking
on the floor above you from the cellar, especially if the floor is
wood. If the zombie's hearing hasn't totally deteriorated, they'll
probably note the sounds of movement and be drawn to it. If they
don't hear you, they will see your flashlight. Let them come to you
in this case. Don't go walking down the steps and let them grab and
bite you from between the steps or from the side of an open
stairway.

You need to maintain your situational awareness of what's going
on outside the house too. Make a point of looking out the windows
of each room when you can. Look for undead in the yard or the
next yard, or the street. It's easy to get in over your head when you
are doing searches. Depending on the radio equipment you have
and the situation, you may have your radio microphone on or off.
When you are doing this stuff with you radio off, it's really easy to
lose track of what's going on with the rest of the team. Check the
windows frequently.

Some teams like the ZKs on the search to work with their radio
microphones open so they can dictate their findings to the radioman
back in the safety of the truck. This has its merits in terms of speed
but I wouldn't do it unless you have police or other encrypted

radios. Raiders have radios too. If you broadcast a good find in the clear, the raiders might grab it before you get back with the recovery team.

Be aware that taking personal supply requests from private citizens is a violation of your contract as a ZK and can get you in a lot of trouble. All the cigarettes and alcoholic beverages that seem to make their way to the black market in Live E-town aren't walking in on their own. When pickings are slim, nobody likes to go back empty handed, but it looks really bad when you were sent out for medicine and you came back with porn magazines. If you want to do that stuff, and your captain will permit it, do it on your day off. If you get caught freelancing on company time, you could end up getting whipped; likewise if I catch you with Nutella. All Nutella in the Dead Zone is mine. I called it.

Before you search, you need to clear. Open doors are neither a good nor bad sign, but always be on your guard when entering a structure. Blondie and her BFF were bit and died inside this secured out-building and remained until we arrived 16 months later. FYI, the .44 magnum over-penetrated. It passed through the wall and wrecked the sun roof motor on an otherwise excellent Isuzu Trooper SUV parked outside.

This is usually a bad sign. Get out at the first hint of movement.

ZK, feed thyself. As long as the cans aren't bulged, they're good to eat.

Make a point of looking out the window when you are inside a structure so you aren't surprised by unexpected callers. You may not notice the undead that are still, but they often notice you when you pass.

Extermination

Killing Zombies in the Dead Zone is a ZK's business. It's his bread and butter; the thing he gets up in the morning for. What kind of odds are we up against? Consider this. Before the apocalypse there were about 4,360,000 people in Kentucky. Most of them became undead or were consumed by the undead. About 1,300,000 of those people lived in the Louisville metro area just to the north of Live E-town. The majority of them, undead and living, were burnt to ash in the incendiary bombing early in the apocalypse. After that, we might conclude that no more than 3,000,000 undead Kentuckians remained, a third of them concentrated in the major cities and the rest spread out in smaller towns throughout the state. Some factors supporting that as the upper limit are the Ohio River forming a natural obstacle to the north and some pretty rugged terrain throughout the state limiting mobility of the undead. On top of that, some of the undead seem to stay put where they died.

There are plenty of other factors that make the 3,000,000 undead figure nothing more than a scientific-wild-ass-guess. For example, we know that a lot of the undead do move around, and move in big groups. Live E-town was nearly overrun by waves of undead from the north and northeast. We know they will follow prey, human or animal. I believe, and I'm not alone, that the undead will also follow each other. That means when a zombie senses, or thinks he senses, something to eat and begins pursuit, others see him and follow. Before you know it, you have every zombie in sight following and you can have a huge herd of the undead just moving around in any direction. I've seen this. I don't think anyone can know how many herds of undead have wandered in or out of the state from the south and east. We are always on the lookout for them.

One way or another, there are a lot of undead around. A big part of our job is to reduce that number to zero. To do this we have to fight smart. If we don't, we die. Knowing where the undead are at any given time is critical. Our patrols on land, air and river, are constantly watching the Dead Zone.

We are always outnumbered and usually vastly so. When we fight we need every advantage we can get. The most important one is being able to pick our battlefield. Once we spot a dangerously large group of undead, we'll make plans to direct them into prepared positions that protect us while channeling and containing them. This is usually done with pre-existing man-made or natural obstacles that we reinforce as necessary. I've done it on town streets, in large buildings, fenced parking lots and in ravines. We packed these traps with flammable material. Usually we use brush wood which burns fast and hot, especially when dry. It's important to have plenty of real fuel in the trap because the undead by themselves are not highly flammable. How well they burn depends a lot on how much body fat they have. Once the undead are contained and struggling around in our kindling and fuel, we light them up with Molotov cocktails. *(By the way, if you don't contain them, the burning undead can wander about setting everything on fire.)* Fire is the most important weapon we have that can deal with large numbers of the undead. You don't necessarily have to completely burn them up. All you really need to do is get the brain tissue hot enough so that what little that still works gets cooked. Extra points if you get the liquid in their brain sacks so hot it boils and the steam pops open their skulls.

We've got a few hundred of these traps identified around the Dead Zone and on the perimeter. The biggest ones are in sections of forest and ignited by air. We cut firebreaks to both contain the fire and the undead.

Crushing is another effective extermination method. This is a close in defense and works best on flat ground or hard surface roads. You may recall that when clearing the roads we used rows of abandoned cars to create walls on the sides of the roads and to create funnels and channels in open ground. When the undead are drawn into these channels, they have great difficulty escaping and they will pack in like sardines. We'll crush them under the tracks of bulldozers, military armored personnel carriers and anything else with tracks or big rollers that we can use. The drivers and defensive gunners on the heavy equipment are protected in armored cabs with plenty of food, water, ammo and fuel. All of this equipment drinks a lot of diesel so its use is limited to action in the immediate vicinity of Live E-town. As the undead are crushed flat, more pour in to take their place in the channel until the herd is thinned to the point that it's inefficient to crush them. Then we'll take them out with gunfire or draw them to the edges of the channel and kill them with axes or steel pipe.

Winter is the season when the advantage briefly shifts back to humanity. We make the most of it. We know that the undead have no organ function. Their lungs don't breath, their hearts don't beat, their blood gradually congeals and they don't turn up on infra-red cameras or vision equipment because they have no body heat. No body heat means they have nothing to keep them from freezing solid when the temperature drops below 32 degrees and stays there long enough.

Kentucky is the south, so unfortunately we don't have long deeply cold winters all that often, but the last one we had was. It was pay-back time. We used it to thoroughly sweep the close-in farmland and gained enough territory inside the new perimeter to insure we could grow the food we need to keep everyone from starving. In the relative safety of the cold, we got out a huge workforce to build new perimeter fences and defenses. I think that cold winter will go down in history as one of the most important factors in Live E-town's survival.

We also launched offensive operations against undead herds we were tracking by air. These operations were round the clock. They had to be. We don't have WAVE 3 meteorologist Kristie Dutton telling us the five day forecast anymore *(though I've heard she survived and made it to Live Westport)*. Not knowing when the cold would give way, we pushed as hard as we could to smash heads, working in shifts and sleeping under guard in heated tents on the battlefield or nearby buildings. The ZKs, Army troops and about 2,300 civilian volunteers killed 75,000 undead last winter at a cost of 29 men, a third of them from heart attack, freezing, car accident or other natural causes. The success of those operations give me hope. If we can hold out long enough and not make any stupid mistakes to lose this war, we will retake this world for the living.

If it's too cold for shorts, it's a zombie.

When they freeze, they fall. As long as they are standing, they are dangerous!

ZK CAT skinners have a hard and technically challenging job. They kill a lot of zombies. Now all these machine cabs are protected with armor and expanded metal mesh. It was really dangerous duty in the early days when there was nothing between the operator and the undead.

The ZK Code of Conduct

I was raised in the Catholic Church and my values and beliefs were formed there when I was very young. To this day, I never miss a mass. My faith is at the core of my being and it's why I do what I do. Now some would say, "How could that possibly be? You are a really bad person. You cut off a man's hand for touching your ponytail and made people eat cat turds and threw someone down a well." That is true. However, bad people need God a lot more than good people. Imagine how I would be if not for the moral guidance of church. My point is that we need guidelines to live by in this awful new world if we are going to maintain our humanity and the ZK Code of Conduct is part of that. When you sign up for this outfit you agree to abide by the code. The code specifically proscribes nine activities which I will list and illuminate for you in hopes of preserving or improving if necessary your moral character by setting out clearly my expectations for your behavior while a ZK. The forbidden activities are:

- **Murder of a living human being defined as killing without cause.** *(We do a lot of killing. Try to remember you aren't God, only a perfect instrument of His will. Whether you believe in God or not, Hell is waiting for you if you try to usurp His glory. Furthermore, owing somebody money is not "cause".)*
- **Banditry against a living human being or this government to include surreptitious theft of property.** *(If it isn't yours, don't take it. If it's mine… God help you if you take it. Follow this rule outside of the Dead Zone and you should be alright.)*
- **Assault of a living human being defined as a physical attack without cause.** *(Keep your hands to yourself. If you are messing with another person's spouse, expect a punch in the face. Take that punch without complaint because you have it coming.)*
- **Destruction of the property of a living human being or this government.** *(If you become an asshole after a few drinks, you better not drink.)*
- **Fraud against a living human being or this government.** *(Selling dead AA batteries is fraud!)*

- **Slavery, defined as the ownership of a living human being.** *(We despise our enemies for doing this so how could we tolerate it here? Unless... those held against their will and forced to work are your own minor children. Then it's probably ok.)*
- **Rape or sodomy of another living human being or the undead.** *(Yikes! What the heck is wrong with you...we kill raiders for doing this stuff.)*
- **Organizing or engaging in any sort of spectator zombie fighting whether or not gambling is involved.** *(Ok, admittedly this can be a lot of fun when you get a captured Bardstown Baller in there but it might seem barbaric through civilian eyes. We do kill raiders for doing this with survivors after all.)*
- **Usury defined as money lending for profit.** *(I actually don't know anybody who has ever done this. Most ZKs can't seem to hold onto money from one paycheck to the next in order to have anything to lend. If you do, don't lend it for profit. It would be shabby to do your friends that way. Seems like a good way to catch a stray bullet on patrol too.)*

All of these activities are pretty reprehensible and fortunately very few ZKs have been involved in them. We've had some real roughnecks in this organization in the past and still do. I'll be the first to admit that some ZK's do bad things and I blame their officers for letting them get away with it. It's time to realize that you don't get a free pass for mayhem because you put your life on the line in the Dead Zone. New scumbags need not apply, and present scumbags should tender their resignation or clean up their act.

Little kids in Live E-town want to be ZKs when they grow up. You must be a fitting model for them. If you do that, you'll certainly be conveying the right message to the survivors we encounter in the Dead Zone. Nobody says you have to become a good person, just look and act like one when you wear the ZK patch.

Live E-Town: Like it or not, this is our society now.

The zombie plague changed the human relationships we share today in a lot of ways that we never considered while we were fighting for our lives. I try to look at these changes through the lens of my memory of what things used to be like. The old world seems so distant even though it's only been gone two years. We're still eating its canned food and using its manufactured goods. The material things remain the same but the human beings are different now. For our civilization, I think some of these changes are for the better. Some changes I can't define yet as good or bad. Things are just different than they were before. Other changes I think are not so good, or at the very least irritating to me.

Better:

- Racism has diminished greatly. I've been called a "Chinese bitch" only once in the past two years. *(I am not even Chinese.)* I rarely hear the words nigger, cracker, dot head or spic . The fact that you are a living human being is more important to most people than your race. There's a common bond among most Live E-town citizens. Just about everyone has had to fight to stay alive, either to get to Live E- town or to keep it from being overrun when half a million undead were pressing up against its outskirts.
  Whatever truth there may have been to the old stereotypes, they obviously don't fit too well anymore *(although I am good at math).* For example, nobody would think of saying that blacks are lazy anymore. There is so much evidence to the contrary it would be ridiculous to make a statement like that. Nobody is allowed to be lazy in this new world. Lazy people are already dead. Everyone has to pull their weight growing food, fixing roads, storing supplies, issuing clothes, improving the defenses, etc. Live E-town is no welfare state. You work hard and work together or we all die. Don't work hard enough and you'll probably get your ass kicked by everyone else until you are earning your keep. There are still a lot more jobs that need to be done than there are men and women to do them.
- Obesity is no longer a national health crisis. "You only need to run faster than the fat guy" is a dark joke that I still

hear regularly. There is a lot of truth in that. You don't see a lot of over-weight people anymore. We don't have fast food *(or any other)* restaurants and the food supply is not what we want it to be. Food is still rationed by the Mayor's Council and probably will remain rationed for a long time to come. I never went hungry because, like most ZKs, I can go out in the Dead Zone and find my own food. I know there were plenty of times that the people in town were hungry.

- There are a lot of babies around. It seems that the apocalypse either kicked people's libidos into overdrive or deeply suppressed them. Contraception wasn't a high priority and/or immediate violent death seemed fairly likely so lots of couples didn't bother with birth control. It's a good thing in the big picture because children represent hope and we need hope. Practically minded people say we need to increase the ranks of the living if the human race is going to survive and get back on top. A woman cannot get an abortion. The hospital won't do it and doctors are forbidden to. It takes a zombie apocalypse to kill off a few billion people before they stop murdering their own unborn children. Go figure.

Different:
- In the absence of a legal structure supporting and enforcing it, marriage and divorce are in decline. Nobody has married civilly or divorced in town since the apocalypse. If couples don't get along, they just go their separate ways, usually with one being unceremoniously locked out from their shared residence. The displaced half goes and finds a new place, usually his slutty girlfriend's, or petitions the Mayor's Council for the use of an empty house or apartment. The Mayor's Council can be brought in to rule on the separation of property, if any. The Mayor's Council takes 20% of the couple's property as a tax for this service. The Council can also move children to new homes if parents cannot amicably separate or it is believed the children will not be protected and cared for adequately. These consequences encourage couples to work their problems out. There are plenty of people who will take children.

Keep in mind that probably half of the "families" in Live

E-town are transplants from other areas and perhaps half the children here are being raised be people who aren't their biological parents. When the worst of this was going down, there was enough loss and heartbreak for everyone. Families were destroyed and then remade from the material on hand. Children needed parents. Parents, mourning the loss of their children, made orphans their own and loved and protected them like their flesh and blood.

It was a little more complicated for widowed wives and husbands to find new spouses. New "marriages" emerged from the shared hardship of survival. These new bonds between people could be as strong as the old ones, but they were different. Consider the value of trust in a relationship. Multiply that by the factor of the value of your life. When a couple keeps each other alive, it builds a comradeship not unlike that shared by soldiers in battle. Add to that the slightest amount of physical attraction and you have a feeling they may have never had for their pre-apocalypse spouse. Of course, take away the stress of staying alive day to day and they become the same inconsiderate asshole/bitch they were before and you either deal with it or go your separate ways.

Worse:

- Though an abomination, a sort of polygamy is not uncommon now. Sometimes a woman will have two or more "husbands "or vice versa.
- It seems to me that everybody thinks they can hit on everybody else, any time, any place. I am propositioned *(by men and women)* every time I go to Live E-town, including when I'm at mass which enrages me. I started wearing a wedding band thinking that might reduce the unwanted advances to a manageable level. They actually increased. Hot though I may be, and unfortunately especially appealing to Asian fetishist perverts, I know it's not just me getting all this attention. Many women I know have the same observations, though they don't seem to mind as much. Personally, it offends my sensibilities. I was raised and educated in the Catholic faith and remain a member of Opus Dei. It seems grossly inappropriate to me that everyone should be so horny in the end times. Think about it. Do you

really want to be engaging in acts of fornication and sodomy when Christ returns? That's like a million times worse than your parents walking in on you and your date in high school. Maybe a billion times worse.

• Furthermore, a majority of men now believe the old rules of staying in your league no longer apply. There is certainly little, if any, apparent evidence that hotties are pairing with creeps, dweebs or losers but the propositions keep coming like a zombie horde. The apocalypse seems to have emboldened these poor specimens of manhood. I just politely decline their offers to show me their giant one-eyed-wonder-worm *(so lame),* lick my butt like an ice cream *(gross!)*, and other perversions too numerous to list. Nobody ever asks me to play Scrabble *(my favorite)* so I spend my free time in town teaching the kids at church, the same thing I did with my free time before the apocalypse.

• This is no country for old people. The surviving population is almost devoid of the elderly. People over age 70 are hard to find. There were cases early on when the elderly were preemptively murdered by their neighbors who feared they would die of natural causes at some indeterminate time in the near future and then present a threat to the living. The elderly could not defend themselves or escape from the undead as well as younger people so very few of them came to Live E-town as refugees. For the most part, the older people in town resided here before the apocalypse.

My culture treated our elders with great respect. As a ZK you have to save the most valuable survivors first. In a bad situation, that often means leaving the old and infirm behind in favor of the young and strong. It is deeply unsettling to me to do this. Especially in cases when I have the feeling that the people we save are less worthy than those we have to abandon. I have seen grandparents suicidally distract the attacking undead so their younger relatives could escape. There can be no greater act of love than this selfless sacrifice. I believe that God awaits them in heaven with open arms. I respect them. I salute them. I try to kill them before they have to suffer being torn apart.

The original artwork for the seal of Live E-Town. It was colored with child's crayons. That's me on the right.

Excerpt from the introduction *of **Live E-Town in the Zombie War: A Military & Political History*** researched and written by Frank Jardim

From the facts we know in the Spring of 2014, it is estimated that around 10% of the regional human population survived the Zombie War and perhaps half of those lost to the ranks of the undead were lost in the first weeks of the contagion's release. Elizabethtown and Hardin County had a survival rate closer to 50% thanks largely to geographical good fortune. Louisville was hit first and fell into chaos so quickly that regular U.S. Army units deployed en-mass from Fort Knox in the first days to try to restore order. Not knowing what they were dealing with, the Army returned their wounded to Ireland Army Hospital on the base and two days later all of that facility was overrun from within with contagion spreading to surrounding Radcliff, Westpoint & Muldraugh.

The remaining military units in the area, which included Kentucky Air National Guard, retreated south of Radcliff and set up a perimeter. Much credit is due to Col. Timothy Reed, commander of the surviving Air Force elements, and his pilots and flight crews. Colonel Reed alone made the decision to destroy Louisville, Fort Knox and the former population centers between, on a north-south axis, with napalm. The men and women under his command bore the painful burden of carrying out the attacks on what were in some cases their own communities. Who can forget the haunting photograph of the late Captain Nick Panagakos sitting in his cockpit with tears streaming down his face as his plane sat on Addington Field re-arming for his eleventh sortie.

After nine days of desperate combat on the ground it was apparent that humanity was on the verge of annihilation unless the odds could be evened up. Surely hundreds, perhaps thousands of survivors were killed in the air attacks but in the short term it allowed time to regroup and consolidate a defense. The undead were hemmed in by the rivers to the west and north, and had their number not been reduced dramatically through the incendiary attacks, they would have flowed south in overwhelming numbers. As it played out in the following weeks, it was a very near thing. The scientific mind can have difficulty embracing the metaphysical, but I cannot help but feel that it is little short of a miracle we are here today to tell the tale.

A second miracle might be found in the conduct of Kentucky Army National Guard (KYARNG) units operating to the east. Very few of these men and women are alive today to tell their story but what is known is heart rending. It appears that contagion reached Bardstown shortly after it hit Fort Knox. An injured Fort Knox civilian worker returned to his home and ultimately infected his community. The zombie contagion was contained at first by quick and draconian actions by the military on the fifth day of the outbreak. The entire surviving population of Bardstown was evacuated and secured on the grounds of the water treatment facility on State Route 62. The facilities defenses were beefed up with concrete obstacles, double perimeter fencing and even a moat. This improvised fortress was intended to protect the population until they could be transported to a safe area.

Having circled the wagons, the remaining military reinforced by civilian volunteers counterattacked into the city proper and some of the surrounding areas. Losses were heavy especially along Route 282. The undead ultimately won Bardstown (now Dead Bardstown) but their numbers were so reduced that they presented little threat to the tens of thousands of survivors gathering in Elizabethtown. The remaining Bardstown fighters retreated there and were swept up in the epic battles of the following weeks.

The ironic and tragic epilogue to the fighting around Bardstown was the loss of the evacuation center there. Somehow, an infected refugee was admitted and what was once a fortress to protect the living became a prison for the undead. What few details that are known from the 126 people who escaped are too horrific to relate. It was sealed with over 2300 souls inside.

The actions of the KYARNG and the civilian volunteers fighting North of Bardstown had strategic implications. They lost the city and most of its population but they blocked the flow of undead southward along Route 282. That prevented huge numbers of zombies from falling on Elizabethtown from the east which is an important consideration in view of the intensity of the zombie attacks from the north on the I-65 Corridor in the following weeks. A two front defense against attacks of that magnitude would have been impossible. .

Last year the eastern perimeter was pushed out five miles beyond I-65. That flank was secured with Outposts #4, 5, 6 and 7 running north to south on the edge of the Dead Zone. Outpost #7 stands at the egress of the Live Bardstown-Munfordville Road from the forest. It may interest the reader that United States President-elect Andrew Jackson traveled down it on the way to his inauguration in 1828 and actually spent the night in the solid brick house where mercenary zombie killers now execute their security duties. The road itself is little more than a wagon trail and was abandoned as a main thoroughfare for at least a century. When the zombie apocalypse hit, and almost every car hit the road, the main routes became clogged with traffic, wrecks and soon after, the undead. I-65, Bluegrass Parkway, 31W and 31E and many state and county roads were nearly impossible to traverse by car and extremely dangerous to travel on foot. To be on those roads invited attack from the undead, and frankly, still does.

In the apocalyptic era, many old, and nearly forgotten, roads came back into use. Some, like the Bardstown-Munfordville Road, were very thinly populated. Those that dwelt along its meandering path were few, mostly farmers, and the number of infected were manageable. Along the main roads a traveler could encounter herds of the undead at any moment. Travel on the old roads greatly increased ones chance of surviving the journey. It wasn't long after the apocalypse that anything relatively free of the undead was referred to as "Live" and Bardstown-Munfordville Road became Live Bardstown-Munfordville Road. Almost immediately it got the off-color nickname LBM Road. It may come as a surprise to some that it was not harrowing, undergarment soiling, encounters with the undead that earned it that nickname. It was the living that terrorized its travelers. Rival survivalist groups fought viciously for control of it.

Those days were short lived as survivors from the region as far north as Louisville congregated and heavily fortified Elizabethtown. That quiet and inconsequential rural metropolis emerged in the post apocalypse era as Live E-town. This new enclave of humanity was something more akin to a medieval walled city surrounded by thick masonry walls, earthworks, barricades and fences. Initially, universal conscription provided a garrison to defend it.

These draftees fought to the limits of their abilities and their heroic sacrifices represent one of humanity's finest hours. However, it became apparent to most, that valuable and irreplaceable human capital was being lost without which there could be no survival for mankind. Realistic strategic objectives were set only after an agriculturalist faction, formally of the surrounding counties, wrested control of the leadership from urban bureaucrats in a relatively bloodless coup.

Under the agriculturist government, virtually all offensive actions against the undead were eventually handled by mercenary zombie killers. The extreme efficiency of these intrepid men and women secured desperately needed farm lands, grazing lands, and livestock insuring a steady food supply for the survivors assembled in Live E-town. The zombie killers have surely drawn a great deal of attention lately for their more colorful, non-government, private-party business transactions. However, it must be remembered that the majority of them were, and are, the means by which Live E-town stays alive. They patrol the perimeter lands and watch the movements of the undead; keep the roads clear that connect the city to its food supplies; create the diversions that draw zombie herds away from the city; scour the dead-zones for required manufactured goods and rescue the lost.

Greeting Mr./Ms.

   As the mayor of Live E-town, I welcome you to the ranks of our fair city's contract zombie killers. You join a team of resourceful fighters whose contributions to humanity's survival are both many and storied. I expect that you will conduct yourself in a manner consistent with this honorable group during such time your contract remains in effect, both inside and outside city limits. Remember that even when you are in the Dead Zones, you are a representative of this community and must refrain from any actions that would bring discredit to it. For clarification, some of those prohibited actions are:

- Murder of a living human being, defined as killing without cause.
- Banditry against a living human being or this government, to include surreptitious theft of property.
- Assault of a living human being, defined as a physical attack without cause.
- Destruction of property owned by a living human being or this government.
- Fraud against a living human being or this government.
- Slavery, defined as the ownership of a living human being.
- Rape or Sodomy of a living human being or the undead.
- Organizing or engaging in any kind of spectator zombie fighting whether or not gambling is involved.
- Usury, defined as money lending for profit.

   Evidence of any of these action can result in disciplinary proceedings up to and including, loss of pay, fines, cancellation of your contract or in extreme cases even imprisonment with hard labor or immolation.

   Through God alone, Live E-town persists as a bastion of mankind. We remain surrounded by enemies, not unlike Jerusalem in the book of the Prophet Isaiah. Through God's hand Jerusalem was protected from the Assyrians who conquered and laid waste to all the surrounding nations. So are we protected by God. You are His instrument. Please try to act accordingly. I pray for your success.

Your assignment is:

Your report date is:

Your supervisor is:

                                      Respectfully,

                                        Max White
                                        Mayor, Live E-town

This is the welcome letter from the mayor's office all ZKs get when they sign on with the city. Rules, rules…lots of rules.